Deathly silence gripped the cha~~ ~~
Garlotte quietly seetl
had publicly sided with Victor
indicated his stance. Now, the ~~p~~
was making a public show of deli
likely, should have been conveyed

"What trouble?" the prince ask   ~~y~~. ~~i~~ie could hardly
put the genie back in the bottle at this point.

"Violence," said Isaac ominously. "Gunfire in the streets—
more than is usual even for *the capital*." He spat out the last
words with distaste, as if the very idea of that city occupying a
loftier position than Baltimore offended him.

A din of an order to put all the previous disruptions to
shame immediately erupted. Cries of "The Sabbat! They're
here!" and, "Kill them! Kill them all!" filled the room.

"Jesus long-haired Christ!" shouted Roughneck.
"Washington has fallen!"

Next to him, the Quaker broke into despondent tears. "I
knew it would happen….knew it would happen…."

Victoria tried to harness the sudden surge of adrenaline.
"You see? This is what I…" But no one was listening.

The Anarchs were boiling over. They stomped up and down
in outrage, ripped seats from their moorings, pounded on one
another's shoulders, and in general whipped each other into a
collective frenzy.

"Stinkin' bastards!"

"Kill every last…"

"Gonna split open their…and pull out their …and kick in
their…"

VAMPIRE

THE MASQUERADE

CLAN NOVEL
VENTRUE

BY GHERBOD FLEMING

WHITE WOLF

part one:
hospitality

Friday, 25 June 1999, 11:30 PM
Pier 13, Port of Baltimore
Baltimore, Maryland

The limousine cruised slowly through the port facilities. What light there was failed to penetrate the tinted glass but reflected sharply from the spotless chrome and other well-polished surfaces of the vehicle. The automobile eased to a halt before the gangplank of a small freighter—small compared to the mammoth beasts that every day graced the docks, loading and unloading tons upon tons of cargo. The night-time skeleton crew of warehouse workers paid little attention to the limousine. It was not so rare that a wealthy investor or ship owner made a personal inspection of his holdings, though the hour was somewhat peculiar.

One of the car's rear doors opened. "Wait here," said Alexander Garlotte before climbing from the air-conditioned interior out into the salty night air. His deathly white face shone like a beacon in contrast to his thick, raven-black beard and the hair that draped over his shoulders. He stood tall, like an English lord of centuries past surveying his manor; the limousine next to him took the place of a powerful and well-groomed charger. Most wealthy gentlemen would have harbored misgivings about frequenting this part of Baltimore so long after dark, but Prince Garlotte was unconcerned. This was his city.

He climbed the gangplank onto the ship, *El Vigoroso*, a Peruvian freighter that had entered the harbor without proper papers. Straightening out such documentation problems, with the bureaucratic hoop-jumping that it required, could take at the very least weeks, and Garlotte's people in the customs office and the port authority were in no hurry to expedite the matter. In the meantime, Garlotte had found a suitable use for ship and crew—a sad collection of unpaid and malnourished sailors, who were simply glad not to be turned away to starve on the high seas.

All was quiet on board. Garlotte made his way inside and along a few tight corridors to the cabin that had served as the captain's quarters. The prince rapped lightly on the door.

"Come in."

Her voice was like the music of the tides, though Garlotte could hear an unaccustomed edge in her tone even now. He opened the door and gracefully stepped inside. She stood behind a large wardrobe that she'd turned away from the wall to form a dressing screen of sorts. The cabin itself was cramped and unremarkable, badly in need of fresh paint, cleaning, and probably fumigation.

"You were too kind, Alexander," she said from behind the wardrobe.

"Nonsense. I would do anything in my power..."

His words died away as Victoria stepped into view. She wore the elegant, black evening gown he'd had delivered, and the matching velvet gloves that rose to just below her elbows. Not overly formal, no sequins or feathers. As Garlotte had accurately recalled, she needed only finely crafted simplicity to complement a radiant beauty that would outshine any accoutrements.

"My God, you are ravishing," he found himself saying. Victoria smiled demurely with a subtle batting of eyelashes. Garlotte basked in the obvious danger of her appeal. Her considerable beauty was both more and less than it seemed: more than mere physical perfection; less than completely candid. Her mystique was the crux of her powers. This Garlotte well knew. Yet the stirrings of sentiment that her mere presence aroused in him were intoxicating. Passions moved that he had not felt in...well, in many years. He moved closer, like the moth circling an open flame.

"How can I ever repay you for this exquisite gown, Alexander?" she asked.

He slipped around behind her, but then paused. There it was again, the slight tension in her voice that he did not remember from their previous encounters.

"Feasting on the sight of you in it," he said, "is more than payment enough, my love."

My *love*, he repeated in his mind. *How I indulge myself.* Only because he was attuned to the mysterious strain in Victoria's voice did he notice the muscles of her bare shoulders tense slightly at the word *payment.*

She has debts outstanding that must be repaid, Garlotte speculated. Perhaps I can be of assistance; perhaps there is a way to bind her to me. But the prince paused for only a brief moment.

"I have taken the liberty..." he began, as he produced two golden earrings, intricately engraved. He reached around Victoria and placed them in her hand. "Would you do me the honor?"

She turned a ruddy cheek toward him and smiled as she put them on.

"And of course..." he continued, taking the matching necklace and locket from his jacket pocket.

"Alexander, you flatterer."

"I am too smitten by your beauty to offer anything so disingenuous as flattery." He lowered the necklace over her head. The locket was relatively flattened and rather large, about the size of an open palm. Like the gown, it was elegant in its simplicity of form, yet it shared the intricate markings of the earrings. For many women, the locket would be too much; not so with Victoria. Garlotte lowered it against the hollow of her breasts as he fastened the clasp behind her neck. Victoria's skin radiated warmth. The prince breathed in her luxurious fragrance. He had neither touched nor laid eyes upon the necklace in many years. It had belonged to his wife, to the beloved companion of his mortal years, and had been shut away with her effects for quite some time. But he had felt the urge—the desire, the *need*—to bring it tonight. As Victoria turned to face him, Garlotte breathed the sigh of a cleric who had long contemplated sacrilege and was relieved finally to have given in.

She placed a tender hand on his cheek. "Alexander, it is beautiful."

Garlotte felt tears coming to his eyes. He leaned and kissed her lightly on one cheek and then the other. His cold lips burned with her fire.

It was no coincidence that the ship was completely silent aside from the conversation in the captain's quarters. When Garlotte had responded to Victoria's call last night, he'd found her wrapped in robes that concealed her face and body completely. She'd not allowed him to look at her, and she'd barely spoken to him. Hardly characteristic behavior. He'd heard the pain in her voice, the fear, and when she'd refused to be taken to any of his several havens and implied that she needed blood, he'd arranged this out-of-the-way sanctuary for her. Now the crew of fourteen was nowhere in evidence, and Victoria's skin was flushed with vigor. Fourteen men. Could this angelic creature have given herself so to debauchery? Surely she could never have utilized such a volume of blood, though the prince found the idea vaguely erotic.

"Just a moment, Alexander, and I'll be ready to go." Victoria stepped again behind the wardrobe, where she tended to some hidden possession. The slight tension in her voice was the only indication of her previous difficulties.

The prince was aware she'd arrived from Atlanta, but he didn't know how she'd escaped the bloodshed there, or how she'd come to his city. And now, as he heard the locket click shut, and Victoria rejoined him, he refused to broach the subject. He preferred simply to bathe in the nimbus of her glory.

Victoria slipped easily into the limousine and took her seat between Isaac, who was waiting in the car, and Garlotte, who followed her. The prince observed with satisfaction that Isaac stiffened somewhat in Victoria's presence, even before she almost imperceptibly, and certainly with complete inadvertence, brushed against the younger Kindred's leg. Isaac was obviously aware of their guest's charms, and was on his guard.

The childe may be rash, Garlotte thought, *but he's not ignorant.* A subtle irony, however, lay in the fact that, where Victoria was concerned, preparation really meant next to nothing.

"Victoria," said the prince, "may I present Isaac Goldwin, sheriff of Baltimore. Isaac, Ms. Victoria Ash." *Most recently of Atlanta*, he did not add. He would save his barbs for later, when the novelty and heady excitement of Victoria's presence had worn thin.

As Isaac kissed the offered hand, he pointedly ignored the swell of Victoria's bosom as she leaned toward him. The highlights of shadow in the dim interior served only to accentuate the curves of her form.

He thinks he's doing so well, Garlotte thought, amused. Of course, Victoria would be intentionally clumsy in her half-hearted attempts at seduction. A victim confident in his belief that he'd fended her off would be that much easier prey in the future.

"*Sheriff* Goldwin," said Victoria. "I'm so very impressed." A deep—and quite unnecessary, Garlotte noted—breath again brought her bosom to Isaac's direct and deliberate inattention.

Dear God, Garlotte thought, *she'll brain him with the locket if she's not careful.*

"I serve my prince as I'm able," said Isaac.

"Such modesty," said Victoria, patting his knee.

Garlotte resisted the urge to roll his eyes. She was laying it on a bit thick, but her antics would make for a valuable Socratic dialogue with Isaac later. The prince couldn't help but wonder if his sheriff-childe would underestimate the fetching Toreador after this initial introduction, as was no doubt her design. Watching the encounter with a certain amount of detachment, Garlotte appreciated Victoria's stratagem, and also recognized the slightest twinge of jealousy in his own breast as she offered her attentions to another.

My God, she's devious, Garlotte thought, *but she makes me feel alive again.* Though the prince was pleased that Isaac was vigilant against the sway of Victoria's charms, Garlotte was not prepared to deny himself the pleasures, nor the dangers, of her company. *I could turn away from her any time I wanted*, he told himself, knowing the lie for what it was, but not caring.

"What a relief to know that I can step out-of-doors in

complete safety," said Victoria to the young sheriff.

Listening to her banter with Isaac, another undertone of the conversation reached Garlotte's ears. The hard edge that had lined Victoria's voice on the ship, the fear, the vulnerability, was completely absent now. Plying her trade, as it were, she was as self-assured as ever she had been. Perhaps the sport of a young Kindred led her to forget her troubles, or perhaps the vulnerability was a side of her she shared with Garlotte, but not with others. At the thought, he felt hope blossom within himself, but he did not allow it to take hold. Instead, he plucked it from the fallow ground and turned it over in his hand, seeing it for what it truly was—self-delusion. Now he flattered *himself*...but what could be the great harm, he wondered, if he was aware of the fact?

Regardless, the prince had seen and heard enough of Victoria's flirtatiousness with his childe.

"I hope you'll allow me to provide you more comfortable accommodations," said Garlotte to Victoria. His innocent suggestion was mined with unvoiced questions—*What was wrong with you last night? Have you bled dry enough sailors?*—that the prince was too tactful to ask outright. "A suite at the Lord Baltimore Inn, perhaps?"

Victoria turned to him; her brow furrowed and her lip pouted just enough to be tastefully imploring. "But I've imposed on you so already, Alexander."

"Nonsense," Garlotte continued, ever the dutiful host. "Should I send someone for your bags?" He knew full well that the only belongings she had on the ship were the clothes and toiletries he'd sent her, nothing irreplaceable. She'd arrived in his city a pauper, though certainly she could access bank accounts now that she was...recovered.

"I think not," said Victoria. She laced her hand around his elbow. Isaac was forgotten, discarded, for the time being. "You're too good to me, my prince."

"Nonsense."

The limousine made a stately procession around the harbor, from the working docks west and north, then east again along the upper edge of the Inner Harbor, with its grand public and commercial buildings.

"You've done so much with the place since I was here last, my dear," Victoria said admiringly. She paused and gnawed lightly on her lower lip, obviously trying to recall: "There was some unpleasantness at the time, I believe. Was it the Civil War?"

"War of 1812," Garlotte reminded her.

Victoria shrugged. "I suppose you're right. You men always enjoy the wars so much more."

Shortly after midnight, the limousine turned onto Thames Street and came to a stop before the Lord Baltimore Inn. Garlotte assisted Victoria from the car. She stood by the open door for a long moment and admired the eighteenth-century structures overlooking the restored waterfront. The trinket shops were closed, but a handful of pubs still buzzed with music and activity. Victoria ignored these more modern contrivances and focused on the refurbished architecture, the period sailing vessels tied to the pier.

"How marvelously quaint, Alexander. I can tell you've made yourself right at home here."

"Indeed. Fell's Point." He briefly regaled her with a bit of the obligatory history of the area, then began to offer his arm, but stopped. "One moment, my dear."

The prince leaned down into the car, where Isaac quickly perked up after having been ignored for the latter portion of the drive. "Isaac, the ship Ms. Ash was staying on…see that it's taken far out to sea and scuttled."

Isaac reached for his cell phone to make it so.

Garlotte nodded curtly to the chauffeur, who'd been standing unobtrusively by the open door since they'd stopped, then turned back to Victoria. "Shall we?" She took his arm, and side by side they entered the Lord Baltimore Inn.

Movement was still excruciating. It was a struggle for Victoria to keep the grimace from her face as she slid out of the limousine. In standing, the needles of pain—no, the *iron spikes* of pain—had at her anew. She thanked the gods for Garlotte's long-windedness. By her side, as she fought to maintain her composure, he lectured her about the renovated buildings, the old ballast stones that were used to cobble the streets in the historic facsimile, and...well, she wasn't sure what else. His words seemed to run together into one long, monotonous drone. And all the while, Victoria could smell the vital fluid of the mortal driver standing not two feet away, but she was unable to do more than smile and nod politely.

Surely one more would, sate my thirst, she thought, catching sight of the chauffeur in her peripheral vision. But she'd had that same notion on board the ship...again and again and again.

At last, Garlotte extended his arm, and she allowed him to escort her into the inn. The facility was a magnificent reconstruction, full of natural-grain woodwork and hardwood floors, brass fixtures, oriental carpets, and of course the attendants—*employees*, she must remember to call them—were all dressed in period garb. A minor sideshow for the typical tourist or businessman, but for many Kindred, such attention to detail afforded the opportunity to escape the oh-so-confusing modern era and luxuriate in self-delusion. Victoria suspected that Garlotte must spend a great deal of time here.

Partway across the lobby, she stopped, closed her eyes, and drank in the fragrances of her surroundings: A-positive, the bellboy; B-positive, the desk clerk; B-negative, the housekeeper....

Don't I just have the one-track mind tonight, she realized, but she couldn't help it. Her escape from Atlanta had left her debilitated—not the escape itself, but the several nights of her preceding imprisonment. Elford, that Tzimisce fiend, a mockery of humanity, had... She shuddered at the mere thought.

"Have you caught a chill, my love?" Garlotte asked her quietly as he led her toward the elevator and rubbed her shoulder. His fingers were ice against her skin, but she fawned reassuringly at him.

Elford had...mistreated her. Badly. His ministrations had left her damaged in ways she'd been unsure would ever heal. But despite the lingering discomfort, heal they had, for the most part. Enough that she could wear the revealing gown the prince had presented her. The gloves were a fortunate accessory, and luckily the back did not swoop too low. She was continually amazed by the power of blood—the very stuff of life itself—once it entered her undead form. Even so, the sheer amount of blood that had been required had appalled her...afterward, when she realized what she'd done.

But spilt milk, and all that, she thought.

The elevator had buttons for the first five floors. Garlotte inserted a key that allowed access to the sixth and seventh.

"I issued the summons, as you requested," said the prince, turning to business at last.

Victoria, too, set her mind to the matters at hand. She squeezed his arm playfully. "*Invitations,* my dear. Invitations. We're not holding these darlings for trial." As she chided him for his authoritarian manner, her thoughts were ranging in another direction.

Fourteen. There had been fourteen sailors. She could move forward with her plans. The ship's register had listed nineteen crew members, which would have been disastrous, or if not disastrous would at least have caused Victoria to abort her current course of action. The captain, with some gentle encouragement, had admitted to her that he'd fabricated five sailors in the records so that he could draw their wages for himself. Good old-fashioned, South American industry and graft. Victoria had been quite heartened.

Before Garlotte had left her on the ship, she'd asked him to call together whatever Kindred he could, especially survivors and refugees—such as herself—from the Sabbat attacks to the south. Her dear Setite rescuers, before she'd abandoned them at the airport, had told her more of the irresistible attacks that, from nowhere, had swept across much of the eastern seaboard over the past nights. Atlanta, Savannah, Charleston, Columbia—all had fallen in short order. Whatever Kindred had survived—and from Atlanta, as of yet, she knew of none other than herself—would find their previous domiciles patently inhospitable, she imagined. Some might flee west, to Chattanooga, Knoxville or, more likely, New Orleans. But many would head north, especially if they were unaware of the northward progression of the Sabbat forces on their heels. Also likely.

Such forced migration, Victoria knew, would result in chaos—princes were destroyed or, at the least, turned out of their cities; the masses were uprooted and fearful—and whoever managed to reassert order in the midst of bedlam would achieve significant laurels indeed.

So she'd asked Garlotte to call the Kindred together, and he'd done her bidding in this. She would rally the troops, so to speak; she'd selflessly provide herself, refugee in her own right, as the shepherd of lost souls…and they would adore her. They would beg her to lead them. She had been so close to the reins of power in Atlanta, only to have them snatched away by the damnable Sabbat interference. The players had all been assembled and primed. It had been obvious that Prince Benison would either have fallen to Julius, or would have been deposed by the Camarilla if he'd managed to destroy the Brujah archon. Thelonious and Benjamin had come together in an uneasy alliance; the prince's whorish wife Eleanor would have met an unfortunate end, and perhaps taken one of the conspirators with her. The doors to the halls of power would have opened wide, and Victoria would have stridden in unopposed.

If the thrice-damned Sabbat hadn't crashed her party (quite literally), and churned all of her careful preparations to ruin.

More troubling, however, than the failure of her plans, more frightening than the torture she'd undergone at the hands of the vile Tzimisce, was a vague suspicion she couldn't shake from her bones—namely, that she was a mere pawn. True, it was a concern she'd carried with her for many years, and a justifiable worry it was. Just as most mortals were completely unaware of the shadow-society of undead beings who held sway over the night and greatly influenced through mortal agents the events of the day, most Kindred had little to no inkling of the far older and more powerful forces in the world, those who pulled the strings of those who pulled the strings. Victoria was not so ignorant of the elder beings. Not that she had definitive proof… but then no one did. Her intuition in the matter, however, was so strong, so undeniable, that the knowledge passed as a certainty for her.

And so she had long guarded the integrity of her actions and sought to insure that her plans were her own, not the whim of some unseen player in the Jyhad—that struggle of the hidden powers, to whom even the Camarilla and the Sabbat were but mere pieces on the board. Victoria had determined to be unpredictable, to make sure than no person, no creature, could idly count on her to play a certain role in any endeavor. On the surface, those around her expected a mistress of Clan Toreador to be flighty. So much the better if, in fulfilling their shallow expectations, she secured a much deeper purpose.

Even her most simplistic, low-risk, high-yield schemes were subject to the gauge of randomness. As was her custom, she had held her plans in Atlanta up to such a test of independence. The giant embellished doors covered with friezes at the High Museum of Art had served that purpose. Heaven and Hell. Victoria had watched who entered and by which door. Leopold, the pathetic fop, had chosen Hell, and so as dictated by her elaborate formula involving that and other criteria, Victoria entered the gallery through Heaven.

Yet the evening had turned against her, and in a quite dramatic way. Coincidence? Victoria put very little stock in that concept.

Luckily, she changed, discarded, and tried on new plans as easily as she did clothes or lovers, and since her more Byzantine test of randomness had failed her in Atlanta, Victoria undertook a much simpler test to validate or preclude her Baltimore plans. Rather than a complex equation of minutiae, she had determined to rely solely on one unambiguous factor—the number of sailors on the ship; odd or even. If it had been odd, she would have skipped this gathering of Kindred altogether, never mind that she had instructed Garlotte to arrange it. But there'd been fourteen—not only an even number, but equally divisible by seven, the number of clans making up the Camarilla. How much clearer could the result of her test be? Victoria divined that she was destined to rise to greatness leading her fellow Kindred in the aftermath of the vicious Sabbat attacks, the first of which had dashed her earlier plans. So in a way, the destruction of her efforts in Atlanta had led directly to her current opportunity. Perhaps she had merely descended into Hell so that she might now ascend to Heaven.

"Don't you agree, Victoria?"

She looked up at Garlotte for a moment, realizing that she'd completely missed whatever he'd just asked. She patted his arm. "Of course, my dear." It didn't really matter. Garlotte never asked important questions.

The elevator stopped at the sixth floor. Beyond the doors, the corridor was conspicuously lined by a dozen men in tuxedos. Security. Ghouls, no doubt. Garlotte escorted Victoria past them, and though handsome to a man, none of them cut as fine a figure as the prince in his dark, tailored suit. She labored to keep from her face any betrayal of the physical pain that plagued her with each step.

At the far end of the corridor stood double doors behind one final sentinel. This was no ghoul, but Kindred—a disheveled, wild-eyed creature who looked very much out of place in the posh surroundings, despite someone's attempt to dress him up in a blazer and khakis.

"Victoria," said the prince, "may I present to you Malachi, assistant to the sheriff, and respected representative of Clan Gangrel."

Scourge, thought Victoria. It made sense. Obviously, this one was the teeth behind Sheriff Goldwin. Isaac was no enforcer; he would make the political decisions. Probably Garlotte was grooming his childe as his eventual successor, but the dirty work they would relegate to this unfortunate. A Gangrel retainer, if one of the beasts could be enticed to serve, generally proved as loyal as any dog, twice as useful, and more intelligent than most breeds.

Victoria ignored the Gangrel and straightened Garlotte's tie. "Shall we join the unwashed masses, my prince?"

She took his arm again, and they entered the small auditorium, leaving Malachi to close the doors and sniff at the air.

Saturday, 26 June 1999, 1:44 AM
McHenry Auditorium, Lord Baltimore Inn
Baltimore, Maryland

Chaos. Sheer, unadulterated chaos.

The auditorium was more a glorified conference room, modeled after an amphitheater, with five ascending, curved rows of ten to eighteen seats each, and nearly every seat, at present, was filled with a screaming banshee straight from the pits of hell. Or so it seemed to Garlotte. After an hour and a half, the mood of the "conference" was growing only uglier.

"You might see my point," Victoria insisted over the din to one of the Brujah back-benchers, "if you weren't such an obstinate, imbecilic, disrespectful cad."

The young Brujah waggled his tongue through the "v" of his index and middle fingers. The rest of the rabble roared approvingly and took up his gesture as well.

Perhaps, Garlotte surmised, *Victoria is not completely in her element.* One on one, she could undoubtedly wrap any of these whelps around her little finger, stake him out for the morning sun, all only to have him beg for more. In this more public forum, however, with each insurgent supported by his comrades, she seemed somewhat at a loss. Seeing that neither charm nor reason were destined to carry the evening, she had proceeded onward to pure invective.

"Why should we expect any of you to understand, you bilious collection of lobotomized perverts?"

Garlotte stood front and center. Victoria was off to his left, near the edge of the well of the auditorium. She'd initially taken a seat as Garlotte had commenced the conference, welcomed the guests to his city, and proceeded with introductions of the notable attendees. The preliminary niceties having concluded without incident, Victoria had risen and briefly ruminated upon the recent unpleasantness initiated by the Sabbat, and the need for a unified response from members of the Camarilla. When one of the Brujah ruffians, all testosterone beneath his too-tight T-shirt, broke in and voiced his support for "busting the balls" of every Sabbat vampire within a thousand miles, Victoria had questioned the prudence of such a strategy.

"Like we need advice from backwoods refugees who already got their asses kicked," the Brujah had replied, and the discourse promptly deteriorated from that point.

Though Garlotte was unsure why Victoria had allowed herself to be drawn into such an acrimonious and ill-focused debate, he was growing increasingly perturbed with the behavior of the rougher element. Most were Brujah, of course. Generally, they led the existence of Anarchs, roaming freely between Baltimore and Washington, shirking clan responsibilities, and only bothering to show up at Kindred functions when there was trouble to be made or what they considered entitlements to be claimed. To this point, Garlotte had allowed them to express their views unhindered for two reasons: first, he himself was uncomfortable with some of the implications of what Victoria suggested, and he didn't wish to create the impression that he supported her unconditionally; second, to quash the incendiary element prematurely might draw the ire of conference's most notable participant.

Perhaps *participant* was too generous a description. Thus far, Theo Bell had not uttered a word. He sat in the right end-seat on the third row, though as archon to Brujah Justicar Pascek he was entitled to a central seat on the first row. Only partially hidden by his mirrored sunglasses and black, low-pulled baseball cap was the seemingly perpetual scowl on his ebony face. He was a big, muscular man, and his bulky leather jacket and crossed arms heightened that impression. His very presence necessitated restraint in dealing with the other Brujah. Even so, Garlotte's patience was near its limit.

The back-benchers were again directing indelicate gestures

toward Victoria. In their midst, someone began to stomp, and within seconds a score of booted feet had joined in.

Garlotte stepped forward and raised a hand. The uproar quickly died down to a few lingering stomps. One of the less unruly among the Brujah—Garlotte recalled her as Lydia—smacked the offender on the back of the head, and the stomping ceased altogether.

"There are those," said the prince calmly, at the same time his iron gaze bore into the Anarch crowd, "from whom we have not yet heard." He intentionally avoided looking in Victoria's direction—she would be displeased that he had not come to her aid earlier—as he then turned to the other side of the auditorium with a most inviting expression pasted on his face.

In response, Maria Chin, the sole representative of Clan Tremere ordered to the gathering, stood and coolly surveyed the chamber to make sure she had the attention of at least most of those present. The Brujah rowdies were cowed, if not rendered completely reticent, by the prince's intervention. "Ms. Ash," began the witch from the clan's Washington chantry, "you speak of a unified response, or concerted action, but it seems to us that at present we lack a complete assessment of the situation."

Victoria's spirits rose noticeably. "A remarkably insightful statement...at last," she added, glancing toward the upper reaches of the chamber. A collective hiss emanated from that section, but quickly died away with a pointed glare from Garlotte.

"If we are to respond to these incursions of the Sabbat, *as we must*," Victoria insisted, "we must first gather as much information as possible. I imagine you might be able to enlighten us regarding how the Tremere have fared over the past nights...?"

Chin measured carefully the words of her response. No trace of emotion crossed her eastern features. "Like every other clan, we have suffered ...some damage."

Garlotte was not surprised by the vague nature of Chin's answer. The Tremere was not about to reveal to anyone outside her clan the degree to which the warlocks might or might not have been weakened by the Sabbat's attentions. *Victoria must know that*, he thought.

Now another Toreador, and one of Garlotte's own subjects, spoke up. "Certainly no clan has navigated the past week unscathed," Robert Gainesmil conceded. "But how many chantries still function among the aggrieved cities?" he asked more pointedly. "If we are to stand against the beasts, then we first must know where we ourselves stand."

"Screw the warlocks!" one of the Brujah shouted, and a new uproar of support filled the auditorium.

Garlotte waited patiently this time. He also took note of the fact that Gainesmil, a longstanding and staunch supporter of the prince, was supporting Victoria, for whatever good it would do them. The secretive Tremere would not, on the grounds of sect loyalty or anything else, be berated into giving away what she—and more importantly, her superiors—considered to be privileged information.

Chin, meanwhile, remained as unruffled as the plain, gray skirtsuit she wore. The caterwauling of the Anarchs affected her no more than the insinuations of disloyalty to the Camarilla from the two Toreador.

"We agree," said Chin, "that assembling the proper information is vital."

Proper, thought Garlotte. *There's the rub.*

"Do we have a reliable listing of the cities that have fallen?" Chin asked.

"Atlanta, Savannah." The new, deep and powerful voice instantly gained the attention of all present, rowdies in the back notwithstanding. Theo Bell matter-of-factly ticked off the cities on his fingers. "Charleston, Columbia, Greenville, Asheville. Raleigh and Wilmington, North Carolina, fell last night. Norfolk is under attack tonight; the press'll call it labor unrest with the shipbuilders. Communication is broken with Charlottesville and Fredericksburg."

"Dear Lord," Gainesmil whispered in awe at the recitation as he slouched in his seat. "The barbarians are at the gate."

"Bring 'em on!" shouted the same Brujah who'd disparaged the Tremere before. His kin echoed his sentiments. Theo crossed his arms again and returned to his earlier impassive attitude.

Chin resumed her seat as well, now that the focus of the conference had shifted from her perceived recalcitrance to the frightening progress of the Sabbat.

"It should be obvious," said Victoria, seizing the initiative again, "that we must stand against them."

"What exactly do you propose?" Garlotte asked. He had a suspicion, but had heard only generalities so far. "Surely Prince Vitel in Washington and Prince Thatchet in Richmond, and others, are taking the necessary precautions. As am I."

"But can any one prince," Gainesmil interjected, "prepare sufficiently, considering...?" He waved his hand, as if tracing a line of the fallen cities, and looked uneasily back and forth between Garlotte and the again silent Theo Bell.

The prince suppressed a scowl. That his subject would question his ability to protect the city was galling, though it appeared that Gainesmil's blunt questioning stemmed from worry rather than from any desire to damage Garlotte's standing.

"My point exactly," said Victoria. "One by one, our cities will fall—"

"They can't keep doing like they been doing," interrupted Lydia the Brujah. "They don't have it in them."

"They seem to have had it in them so far," Victoria said. "They had it in them enough to kill Archon Julius."

The resulting shocked silence quickly gave way as the backbenchers erupted at this insult. As the rougher element of Brujah hurled unflattering epithets at Victoria with reckless abandon, Garlotte cast a wary glance toward Bell. The leather-clad official of their clan seemed to have taken no umbrage at Victoria's throwing the demise of his fellow archon in their faces. Then again, Bell was notoriously difficult to read.

Victoria somehow made herself heard above her detractors. "This assembly must take responsibility for the resistance to these attacks. We must coordinate a defense. Otherwise, our cities will fall like dominoes."

"Just like South-fucking-east Asia?" ruefully cried an Anarch who, by the look of him, could well have been a Vietnam veteran.

"This isn't supposition," Victoria snapped. "You heard the list; you heard what Theo said." Her implication that the archon supported her position gave the other Brujah pause. "If we don't take action, city after city will fall."

A shabbily dressed, strange old bird with a beard long enough to tuck in his pants, shot to his feet and thrust a finger into the air. "They will never take D.C.!" he asserted. His equally unkempt companion nodded vigorous agreement.

Garlotte was surprised by their sudden, passionate interest. Both of the Malkavians, known only as Roughneck and the Quaker, generally kept to themselves. But the prince also knew that he should never let himself be surprised by *anything* one of the lunatics did.

"I never thought they'd take Charleston," piped up one refugee.

"Or Savannah," agreed another displaced southerner.

"We must take control of the situation," Victoria asserted.

"By what authority?" All eyes turned toward the speaker, Prince Garlotte. Here was the crux of his reservations. Obviously something had to be done, but an arrangement that trampled on his sovereign rights as prince was unacceptable.

"By the authority of necessity," said Victoria. "By the authority of survival. I was in Atlanta. I barely escaped." She cast a glare so cold at the Anarchs that none of them dared defy her or mock her on this point. "I will not be a victim again."

A long moment passed in silence, as every Kindred in the chamber constructed in his or her own mind what it would mean to be a victim of the Sabbat.

But of all of them, Victoria knew. And barely repressed emotion leaked to the surface in her voice: "We must decide what is needed, and then we must call on the clans, the princes, the Inner Circle…." She paused, collected herself. "We must do *whatever* has to be done."

Just then, the double doors at the rear of the auditorium crashed open. Malachi stood to the side as Isaac Goldwin strode into the chamber. He passed, none too gently, several of the Anarchs who had, over the course of the evening, spilled from the seats to block the aisle, and made his way to Garlotte's side.

"My prince," the sheriff bowed respectfully, "there is trouble in Washington."

Deathly silence gripped the chamber.

Garlotte quietly seethed. First, faithful Gainesmil had publicly sided with Victoria before Garlotte had clearly indicated his stance. Now, the prince's own impudent childe was making a public show of delivering information that, most likely, should have been conveyed in private.

"What trouble?" the prince asked grimly. He could hardly put the genie back in the bottle at this point.

"Violence," said Isaac ominously. "Gunfire in the streets— more than is usual even for *the capital.*" He spat out the last words with distaste, as if the very idea of that city occupying a loftier position than Baltimore offended him.

A din of an order to put all the previous disruptions to shame immediately erupted. Cries of "The Sabbat! They're here!" and, "Kill them! Kill them all!" filled the room.

"Jesus long-haired Christ!" shouted Roughneck. "Washington has fallen!"

Next to him, the Quaker broke into despondent tears. "I knew it would happen....knew it would happen...."

Victoria tried to harness the sudden surge of adrenaline. "You see? This is what I..." But no one was listening.

The Anarchs were boiling over. They stomped up and down in outrage, ripped seats from their moorings, pounded on one another's shoulders, and in general whipped each other into a collective frenzy.

"Stinkin' bastards!"

"Kill every last..."

"Gonna split open their...and pull out their ...and kick in their..."

Those who hadn't already, poured from the seats into the aisles. There, for a few moments, they milled in obvious agitation—some shredded the wallpaper with clawed fingers; others tore at their clothes and wailed menacingly—before filtering out through the doorway. A trailing chorus of "Gotta get to D.C. ...gonna kick some ass...stinkin' bastards!" slowly subsided into the distance.

The tension was no less for the absence of the militant faction. Garlotte ignored his sheriff-childe, while Victoria tapped her foot in an irritatingly smug way. Theo Bell had not left with the lesser ruffians; he sat, arms crossed, as inscrutable as ever. The sullen Tremere, Maria Chin, looked as if she'd bitten into a lemon. Roughneck was gone with the Anarchs, leaving the Quaker hiding (not very successfully) beneath a chair. Otherwise, various refugees milled and chattered nervously. They reminded Garlotte of lowing cattle.

Victoria drifted toward the prince. "We must contact the justicars," she said, "so they can notify members of the Inner Circle."

"You don't think they know what's happening?" Garlotte asked.

"I suspect they do. Do I know if they care?" She shrugged. "Am I willing to gamble that they'll send aid unless prodded to it? Are you willing to gamble that—with Baltimore as the ante?"

Garlotte looked over at Bell. The archon, it seemed to him, might be the one to offer some insight in the matter, but Theo appeared inclined to keep his own counsel. Chin, Garlotte knew, was a nonentity among the Tremere; she was a middle-management type sent, because she happened to be nearby, to keep tabs on the other Kindred. If important decisions were to be made, he would have to make them. Victoria stood very close to him. He felt her warmth, caught the glint of light from the locket, his dear wife's locket.

"I will contact Lucinde," he said at last. As much as he hated to call the attention of the Ventrue justicar and the Camarilla powers-that-be to his city—who knew what they might decide?—he would do it. The Sabbat was in Washington. He had to do it.

Garlotte turned away from Victoria. "Isaac, show Ms. Ash to her suite," he instructed his eldest childe, "then come to me. I would speak with you."

Monday, 28 June 1999, 3:47 AM
U.S.S. Apollo, the Inner Harbor
Baltimore, Maryland

The hanging lantern swayed gently from the main support beam. Malachi, much more comfortable in his fatigues and old T-shirt than in formal attire, crouched atop the thick, wooden table and disinterestedly watched Isaac. The sheriff was, for the second night running, manacled to the floor of the cabin, a large sheet of plastic spread beneath him. After all, the prince had spent a considerable amount of money to have the nineteenth-century schooner refurbished, and blood did tend to stain so.

Garlotte sat nearby in a felt-cushioned, straight-back chair, reading the previous afternoon's edition of the *Washington Post* by the light of the single lantern. Reports from the adjacent city were disturbing. The nation's capital had long been infested with a profusion of drugs, prostitution, and violent crime, with much of the nefarious activity precipitated (or at least encouraged) by various undead crime lords. There had always been, however, a certain design, a comforting familiarity, to the mayhem. Not so the past two nights. There was familiarity, but it was far from comforting.

Gang warfare, occasional race riots—these were facts of life, and unlife. Despite what the mortal world tended to believe, such occurrences often were not spontaneous happenings. Usually Garlotte would have received advance notice from the elements arranging such displays. The *usual*, however, had ceased to exist. The Sabbat had seen to that.

Information was filtering north in fits and starts, but from what Garlotte had gathered, the blitzkrieg had started in Atlanta less than a week ago. To most of the world, the seemingly random shootings, the attacks on the High Museum of Art and other edifices around the city, had been some astounding campaign of domestic terrorism. Violent acts elsewhere—more shootings in Savannah; devastating fires in Charleston; a marina explosion in Wilmington—had served only to heighten the mortal paranoia.

But Garlotte knew that the High Museum was a major Elysium in Atlanta, and that two of the other buildings destroyed were Prince Benison's haven and the Tremere chantry. Garlotte knew that several of the city council members shot in Savannah had been pawns, if not actual ghouls, of the Camarilla prince there, and that included among the destroyed sections of Charleston was Prince Purrel's pride and joy, the Battery. Add to that the sudden eruption of nocturnal violence in the shipbuilders' strike in Norfolk. Theo Bell had called that one correctly.

And now, as Isaac had so eloquently reported two nights ago, there was open warfare in the streets of Washington D.C. of a scale that would draw the eyes of the world, and that threatened to spread—with the Sabbat!—north into Baltimore.

Garlotte folded the newspaper and tossed it across the room. He picked up a tin cup, rattled its contents for a moment, then returned the container to its resting place.

"Now, Isaac," said the prince kindly, "I'm going to ask you for the *eighth* time: How is it that you may avoid displeasing me in the future?"

The younger Ventrue drew in a steadying breath, but still his voice quivered somewhat. "I should present important news to you in private, rather than before a crowd."

Garlotte smiled warmly. "Very good."

He turned to Malachi. "Make this one quick." The Gangrel climbed down from the table and took the pair of red-handled wire cutters that had lain there next to him. Garlotte's mind immediately shifted back to the political situation. He barely noticed the screams of his childe, and then the piteous whimpering. Malachi dropped the top digit of Isaac's right index finger into the tin cup with the others.

"Only two more times, and we'll be finished," the prince reminded his childe.

Garlotte had hardly recovered his paper when the knock sounded at the door. From the sound, he knew that Katrina stood on the other side. She rapped sharply, as if she would do violence to the door, not because it stood in her way, but because it *was*. "Enter."

Katrina opened the door and stepped down into the cabin. As she glanced around the cabin, her bright blue eyes didn't even pause on Isaac and his predicament. "Hope I'm not interrupting anything." She ignored Malachi altogether.

"Nonsense," said Garlotte. He extended a hand toward her. "Come to me." She did as he beckoned. *They're always so much more obedient when one of their siblings is in the midst of discipline,* the prince observed. They weren't actually siblings, of course, not in the mortal sense. But they did share a link of blood.

She took his hand. Garlotte loved just to look at her—her eyes; her tiny, pert nose and narrow lips; her strong, wide jaw and pointed chin. Initially he'd been drawn to her by the resemblance to his own, dear Amelia, and when the girl stood silently, he could almost convince himself that he gazed upon his departed wife. If only Katrina wouldn't speak, or defy him, or feel compelled to dress like a common street punk. My *God,* Garlotte wondered, *how many thousand head of cattle have perished so that Kindred might wear leather?*

"You have a visitor," Katrina said, breaking the prince's reverie. "You better see for yourself," she responded to the unvoiced question of Garlotte's raised eyebrow.

Intrigued, Garlotte rose from his seat. "Where is Fin?"

Katrina shrugged. "Probably with his whore."

The prince sighed. *My Amelia would never have spoken so roughly.* He cupped his hand gently to Katrina's cheek. "Ah, my delicate flower, lead me to our guest."

"He's just up on deck."

Garlotte's hand grew tense against her face. His eyes caught her gaze, held it. "Very well. Then you will not have far to lead."

They stepped from the sound-proofed interior of the *U.S.S. Apollo* into the pre-dawn breeze of the Inner Harbor. From Katrina's flippant manner, Garlotte expected almost anyone other than the person who actually waited for him on deck.

"*Vitel.*" Garlotte failed to conceal his surprise.

"Greetings, Prince Garlotte," said Marcus Vitel. He bowed deeply, then rose. "I seek sanctuary in your city."

Vitel was a striking figure: tall, though not so tall as Garlotte; strong features; wisps of gray through his hair; blue eyes, but darker and harder than Katrina's. The visiting prince wore an expensive, tailored gray suit, but it was rather the worse for wear. The left shoulder was torn, and his garments were wrinkled and dusty from head to toe.

Garlotte was beyond the stairs and the handrail, so he placed a hand on Katrina's shoulder. Vitel's presence, and his purpose for seeking out Garlotte, was a dire portent.

"You are, of course, welcome in Baltimore," said Garlotte, "but please, come inside." He indicated a door other than the one through which he and Katrina had just emerged.

"Katrina…" the prince began, but then hesitated. He had a mind that she should serve Vitel and himself. The girl was generally astute enough not to sass her sire in the presence of company, but depending on her manners risked embarrassment. Considering the stature of the guest, Garlotte decided that prudence was the better part of hospitality. "Send for Gainesmil, my dear." He considered ordering her to maintain secrecy, but again, why give the girl orders she would flaunt, when news of Vitel's presence would get out soon enough regardless?

Katrina frowned at the imposition, but not so that Vitel could see her.

At least she didn't roll her eyes, Garlotte thought. *That would have been too much, and I would have been forced to mar that beautiful face. I really shouldn't pamper her so.*

"Dennis," Garlotte called, as Katrina tromped down the gangplank. A stocky, dark-haired man in a blazer and slacks stepped forward from the nearby shadows. His presence was not noticeable until he moved, yet he was one of several handfuls of security ghouls stationed about the ship and dock.

"Dennis, show Prince Vitel into the sitting room."

Garlotte remained on deck for a short while, watching Katrina move off into the distance. It never failed. He could watch her for hours. The motion of her stride, the way she tossed her hair from her face, so much reminded him of Amelia, despite Katrina's continuous quest to be tougher than she was. Garlotte knew she went as far as to consort with Anarchs. He knew other more disturbing, facts about her, but he held those from his mind.

An important guest awaited his audience.

The prince of Baltimore considered sending for Victoria as well as Gainesmil, but decided against it. One Toreador tonight was enough. Gainesmil, an architect turned city planner and undead lieutenant, had long been a partner in strategizing with the prince and should hear what Vitel had to say.

The exclusion of Victoria was not technically a snub, though it could certainly be perceived as such. Garlotte was not ready to grant legitimacy to this notion of hers that she should be instrumental in fending off the Sabbat. He would allow her a certain amount of influence, and he would savor her charms, but he would hold her in check. There was no need to consult her tonight. Besides, with Gainesmil present, Victoria would learn of what transpired soon enough. That was a Toreador consortium worth keeping an eye on, though not necessarily to be discouraged. Garlotte might yet turn to his advantage Gainesmil's familiarity with their high-profile refugee.

"This is a lovely ship," Vitel remarked. "Is it seaworthy?"

"Oh yes, quite." Their conversation remained among topics of mundane interest, as Garlotte had explained that one of his trusted advisors was en route. "Though I'm afraid I don't take her out nearly often enough. I'm sure you know how it goes— work piles up; something always needs immediate attention, and then—*pfft!*—another decade is gone."

Vitel nodded his assent. "You must learn to take time for yourself."

"Ah, that I could," Garlotte bemoaned his responsibilities. "My, but aren't I being the improper host. May I provide refreshment for you, Prince Vitel?"

"Many thanks, but not at present."

"Then I hope you won't think me rude to partake," Garlotte said.

"Please."

Garlotte signaled, and Dennis brought over a decanter and a single goblet. It was such a tricky matter, Garlotte well knew, entertaining a fellow Ventrue. The host was unlikely to have on hand the guest's proper vintage—unlikely to know what it was, as that was a matter of some privacy among the clan—yet still one was expected to offer. Garlotte filled his goblet with rich, life's blood of English descent. It was a variety growing ever more difficult to keep on hand in this modern era of depressingly widespread mobility, a hardship that might eventually require a reverse migration back to the Old Country. For the time being, however, Dennis and several of the other ghouls contributed to the stock handsomely.

"That was your childe, before, on deck, Katrina?" Vitel asked.

The question surprised Garlotte somewhat. Most Kindred hoarded what knowledge they'd gathered about one another like a miser with a golden tooth. The question itself suggested that Vitel had assembled a dossier on Garlotte and his associates. Of course, Garlotte had done the same for Vitel. But the visiting prince's revelation of knowledge lacked any flamboyance, any sense of one-ups-manship. Strangely enough, the query seemed to be...an innocent question.

"Yes. Katrina," said Garlotte.

Vitel simply nodded. His mood, reserved and polite, turned somber. "I had two daughters...two childer. Now...?" He shrugged, dropped his hands into his lap, and stared at the floor.

Garlotte was again stymied. Did Vitel expect ...*sympathy?* The prince of Baltimore was much relieved when Gainesmil's familiar knock sounded at the door.

"Enter."

Garlotte kept the pleasantries to a minimum. He was anxious to hear from Vitel, and the time before sunrise was growing short. The Washington prince remained sullen as he told of the sporadic fighting that had rapidly metamorphosed into a full-scale invasion.

"It was no Sabbat siege, as we've seen before," he explained. "They knew where to hit, and they hit hard. They must've gathered intelligence for years."

"It sounds far too...*organized* for the Sabbat," Gainesmil said.

"I agree," Vitel said. "I suspect Benison in Atlanta would agree, and Purrel in Charleston...."

"Yes, yes," Gainesmil, in his excitement and apprehension, forgot himself and waved away the prince's litany. Vitel, seemingly deflated, appeared to take no offense, but Garlotte noted the infraction so that he might bring it to Gainesmil's attention later. "There's something else at work here," the Toreador continued. "How could they...?" He considered the coordination that would have been required, the logistics, the strategy. He shook his head sternly. "Impossible. Who could have gathered so much support? Borges? Not bloody likely."

"He would be closest to Atlanta, but I agree. Perhaps Polonia," Garlotte suggested.

"I spoke with the leader," said Vitel. The host and advisor fell silent, waited expectantly. "Sarah Vykos."

"Vykos?" Garlotte repeated. Something wasn't right. "*Sascha* Vykos?"

Vitel cocked his head, then nodded. "That may be right. I had assumed her a Jewess."

"*Sascha* Vykos? I thought Vykos was a *he*." Gainesmil said.

"Depends on the night," Vitel replied sardonically.

"I didn't think she circulated beyond Europe," Garlotte added to the general confusion.

"She does now," said Vitel.

"Regardless of who heads the vanguard," Gainesmil announced, "there's a Sabbat army not fifty miles from here! We must send word to the other princes, to—"

Garlotte raised a hand and quieted his advisor. "Yes, there are further preparations that must be attended to, Robert, but our guest has not had an easy sojourn, and here we've been grilling him before he's rested. Prince Vitel, I invite you to stay on board today, and I promise to arrange more suitable accommodations for you on the morrow."

After Vitel's respectful acceptance, Garlotte snapped at Dennis. "See that Prince Vitel is comfortable."

"Yes, sir."

"Gainesmil, come with me," Garlotte said finally. "I must ask Isaac two more questions before I retire."

Wednesday, 30 June 1999, 1:10 AM
Spring Street
Laurel, Maryland

Fin parked three blocks away and made his way silently through the suburban neighborhood. Normally, he was careful—how embarrassing to be spotted by some half-assed, mortal neighborhood watch—but tonight he was even more so. The Sabbat was in Washington. No Kindred could have failed to have heard the stories. The monsters could be heading north any night. All of Baltimore was in a panic—all the undead, anyway. Even some of the mortals seemed to sense the unrest, although their nervousness was probably in response to the overt bloodshed in the capital, rather than to the jitters of the covert bloodsuckers in their midst. But Fin still wondered if the mortals picked up the scent of fear, through osmosis or whatever. Just like a jumpy cowboy might cause his herd to scatter….

The prince had told Fin not to come here at all, not to go south of Baltimore. If the Sabbat did come north, this would be the main corridor of attack. But that was why Fin *had* to come.

A greater danger to the young Ventrue was probably the roaming bands of Brujah who'd taken up patrolling between the two cities—the Kindred version of a half-assed neighborhood watch.

But this neighborhood seemed genuinely quiet, and Fin continued unhindered to his destination. He slipped past the house without setting off the motion-sensor light—he'd discovered that little gem on his first visit—and stealthily scaled the outside of the garage to the open window of the apartment above. He slipped inside without so much as disturbing the lace curtain, and noted with satisfaction that he had not scuffed his shiny leather jacket.

The young woman sat with her back to him, a book open on the table before her, headphones pumping out music loud enough that Fin could hear it across the room. He had no worry of his light tread giving him away. He moved closer, reached out a hand to her delicate neck.

The instant his icy finger touched her skin, she jumped and whirled with a piercing shriek. Her book flew into the kitchenette. The cord of the headphones somehow got wrapped around her wrist, so that the headset slung around and smacked her in the face.

Fin cringed and tried to shush her: "Morena...Morena..."

The flurry of motion ended. She stood wide-eyed and panting; she clutched a hand to her chest. "Jimminy creepers!"

Fin gave her a few moments to collect her wits, and tried not to laugh at what, with her, passed as harsh language. Laughing would only rile her further.

"You *know*" Morena said, as she extracted herself from the headphones and cord, "there *is* a door."

"Your parents might see me."

"*So?*" She retrieved her book and hunted for her place. "I'm twenty-four years old. They don't keep me under lock and key." She stuck a bookmark in the book then set it roughly on the table. "Of course, I haven't mentioned to them that my boyfriend is a carnivorous spawn of Satan."

"Not carnivorous."

"Oh, that's right. You're on a liquid diet. Mom, Dad—Fin is coming over for dinner. Just wring out that raw steak and he'll be fine."

He was on her before she knew he'd moved. Fin drove her backward and onto the bed, landed on top of her, held down her outstretched arms. Morena finally managed a surprised squeak, but her giggles died in her throat as she saw the look in his eyes—burning, glowing red, hungry.

"It isn't all fun and games," he said.

She took a deep breath, found herself unable to look away from him. "I didn't think *any* of it was fun and games."

"Let me make you like I am. You can be with me forever."
His words were a low growl, menacing, but she could hear the
entreaty just beneath the surface.

"I can't.... I can't just leave all...I have responsibilities...my
parents...my job...my gerbils."

"Your *gerbils?* Holy shit! You're going to give eternal life a
pass so you can be with your fucking gerbils!"

"I need more time."

Fin lowered himself onto her, buried his face in the crook
of her neck and lay there for a long, silent moment. "I can't stay
long," he said at last. He ran his tongue along the path of her
jugular. "I can do it, you know. Whether you want it or not."

Morena pushed him off—he let her—and sat up. "You can.
But you won't."

Fin rolled over onto his back and lay next to her. Nearby, her
gerbils scuttled around in their plastic cage. "You don't want
to be with me," he said. Morena stared at her feet but didn't
answer him. "What do you have to lose?"

"My whole life?"

He sighed. She was right. Just like she was right that he
wouldn't drag her into the unlife of Kindred existence against
her will. Not yet. But his resolve was growing weaker.

"You'd have all eternity...with me," Fin said.

"Then there'll be plenty of time for that later, if I decide."

Or if I decide, he thought.

"I think you'd better leave," Morena said.

Fin ran his finger across her back, traced the vertical path of
her bra strap to her shoulder. He gently pulled her back down
to him. Her head lolled back as he again nuzzled her tender,
bare neck.

"Soon," he said, as she gave herself to him. "Soon."

Saturday, 3 July 1999, 10:34 PM
A private office, the Harrison Building
Baltimore, Maryland

To Prince Garlotte's way of thinking, Marcus Vitel was a worthy beneficiary. The two Ventrue, rulers of cities in such proximity, had been rivals for just over thirty years, since Vitel had come to power upon the demise of Washington's previous prince, Marissa of Clan Tremere. Over those decades, Vitel had enjoyed the greater prestige, global geopolitics being what they were. He had woefully neglected clan affairs and kept largely to himself, yet still others constantly had fawned over him: What would wise and powerful Prince Vitel think of this; what of that?

Not that Garlotte was bitter.

However little he trusted Vitel, or however much the prince of Baltimore was galled by the unseemly, sycophantic behavior of those within Clan Ventrue and beyond, Garlotte rested more easily knowing that a fellow clanmate, rather than a Tremere witch, held the reins of power in the District of Columbia.

And now, after thirty years of rivalry, Vitel was almost completely dependent upon the obviously superior stewardship of Garlotte. *Ah, perhaps there is justice in this lifetime,* Garlotte thought. As long as the lifetime in question spanned several centuries.

None of these thoughts broke through Garlotte's studied demeanor of interest and concern, but surely Vitel, seated just across the desk in this quiet office of Garlotte's, knew. Surely Vitel knew that, despite the Ventrue custom of extending succor to a clanmate in need, his host was compiling a long list of favors granted—a list of which Garlotte, in a hundred polite and unassuming ways, would never tire of reminding Vitel.

Currently, less pleasant matters demanded Garlotte's attention. "The governor wisely agrees with me," Garlotte continued with what he and Vitel were discussing, "that it is only fitting that he offer the use of Maryland's National Guard, considering the scope of lawlessness in Washington."

Vitel considered this for a long while. The expatriate prince had largely kept to himself since arriving in Baltimore. Though Garlotte had to concede that six nights, for a Kindred, was a paltry amount of time to grieve for childer lost, he nonetheless felt that prudence demanded he make use of any resources still available to Vitel that could bolster Baltimore's resistance to the Sabbat.

"Why not encourage the introduction of federal troops?" Vitel asked finally. "They would be more reliable."

"More *disciplined*," Garlotte, raising a finger, corrected him, "but for our purposes also more difficult to influence. Unless you have more connections within the Pentagon than one might reasonably expect...?"

Vitel shook his head almost imperceptibly. He appeared somewhat recovered since his arrival in the city, thanks mostly to the replacement of his torn garments with a new tailored suit. But still he retained some of the stunned or shell-shocked bearing that had accompanied his displacement, as if it were a struggle for him to remain fully engaged with those around him.

He seems so...defeated, Garlotte thought. Of course, no one had enough highly placed moles within the federal military to reliably influence large-scale troop deployments for any length of time. Garlotte would have been shocked if Vitel did—almost as shocked as if Vitel had admitted as much.

"So you see," Garlotte continued, "the state troops will best suit our needs. The governor is ready to deploy them. All that remains is for the mayor in Washington to accept the offer."

"The mayor or the Congressional oversight committee," said Vitel, still seeming to pay only half attention. "May I...?" He gestured toward the phone on Garlotte's desk.

"Please do."

"Secure line? Good." Vitel punched in a number, and did not have to wait long. "Good evening, Senator. Forgive me for disturbing you at home.... Yes, Senator. I'm *acutely* aware of what's happening...."

As Vitel spoke, Garlotte could see the fire creeping back into his rival's eyes. The sight was at the same time heartening and alarming—heartening because Vitel in his right mind, resourceful and insightful, was much more valuable in defending Baltimore; alarming because Vitel in his right mind, devious and cunning, might seek to remedy the loss of an old city with the acquisition of a new one.

"If I remember correctly," Vitel was saying into the phone, "your friends on the District oversight committee owe you several favors? And I believe they are already on the verge of declaring a state of emergency and relieving the city officials of control.... Yes, yes. I would appreciate your encouraging them in that direction. Best for everyone, don't you think?"

Garlotte noticed that Vitel was careful not to mention names, not the senator's, not the "friends" on the oversight committee. Probably Vitel had dialed through an intermediary exchange or phone bank as well, though Garlotte would certainly examine the records later.

"Yes, that's correct," said Vitel. "The governor is going to offer the Maryland National Guard. It's imperative that the oversight committee accept this offer. And a city-wide curfew is advisable also. How long can we reasonably expect these measures to be authorized for?" Vitel listened, nodded. "Yes. I understand. I know you'll do your best.... Pardon me.... Yes. I've heard your name mentioned as a vice-presidential candidate.... What do I think? I think your services are far too valuable in the Senate. Goodnight, Senator."

Vitel hung up the phone. Already the fire was beginning to fade from his eyes as the thrill of the deal receded and grief and loss reasserted themselves. "Thirty days. The troops will go in. State of emergency, curfew. But unlikely the oversight committee will authorize beyond thirty days." He tossed up his hands.

Garlotte leaned back in his executive's chair. "It's thirty days more than we had." Grudgingly, he started a new mental list—favors he owed Vitel. Thankfully, it was a much shorter list at present.

"Everything has been so hectic since your arrival, Marcus," said Garlotte, feeling that a change of subject might be to his advantage. "Tell me of your childer." He was sympathy incarnate, wanting nothing more than to ease the pain of his rival.

Tuesday, 6 July 1999, 9:23 PM
A subterranean grotto
New York City, New York

The lamp's flickering light wasn't enough for a mortal to read by comfortably, but Calebros didn't notice. His wide, deep-set eyes were used to near- and total darkness. A good thing, that. Because he spent his nights poring over the reports. Some came electronically via SchreckNET; Umberto brought him the printouts if Calebros didn't feel up to navigating the dank tunnels to the terminal. *I could hook you up a terminal of your own if you got rid of that fossil of a typewriter and cleared off your desk,* Umberto had offered. Calebros had boxed the youngster's ears at the suggestion.

Other messages came via messenger. The largest number of the reports, by far, were of Calebros's own compilation. His sire, Augustin, had taught him the value of putting seemingly extraneous facts together on paper. Often the results were fruitless, but sometimes patterns emerged where none were thought to exist. The crumpled sheet of paper Calebros was currently studying, for example:

6 July 1999
Re: unexplained

6/22 ---- Manhattan, subway tunnel 147:
six workers found dead; newspapers said
bones picked completely clean by (rats)
(and our man at the morgue confirms).

7/2 --- Manhattan, old auxiliary
presses, NY Times: freak flooding of
presses ("dragon's lair") in bedrock
chamber; service elevator fails, one
worker drowns.

Jeremiah inspected—
reports rats in area of tunnel
agitated & aggressive and fat.
Rats near Times presses also
unusually aggressive; not
a problem Jeremiahs had
before.

Thursday, 8 July 1999, 3:02 AM
Governor's Suite, Lord Baltimore Inn
Baltimore, Maryland

The gas logs in the fireplace blazed. Victoria seemed to enjoy a sense of power from being able to command fire to spring forth by simply turning a knob, and all the while not having to get very close herself. She'd turned the air conditioner up to full, so the warmth of the fire was welcome, yet the French doors to the balcony stood open, allowing the breeze off the harbor to play with the floor-length draperies.

"So you've spoken with Vitel?" asked Gainesmil. He brushed a speck of lint from his mint-green silk jabot.

Victoria watched him fussing with the ruffle. "That shirt is hardly worth worrying about, Robert." She stood and walked to the French doors. "Just because it's expensive doesn't mean you should wear it. But then again, some people's taste is all in their mouths."

Gainesmil sat speechless in the face of her rebuke. Earlier, she had treated him quite graciously, even affectionately, but at times Victoria seemed to forget that he was Prince Garlotte's closest advisor, and treated him as merely any other Toreador underling. Gainesmil decided to ignore her comment.

"The prince was quite surprised when Vitel arrived, you know," he said.

Victoria turned her back to him and gazed out over the harbor. "Old news, my dear. That was a week and a half ago."

Gainesmil stuttered but could think of nothing to say. His color rose in consternation. This woman confounded him. Just when he thought their partnership was solidifying nicely, she turned cold and condescending. And if Gainesmil was going to stray from his rewarding loyalty to the prince, he had to be sure of his new ally. Otherwise—unless he was sure of Victoria and of the rewards of pursuing her cause—the risks were not worth his while. He remembered too clearly the tin cup, and how Malachi, at Garlotte's direction, had clipped off Isaac's last two fingertips. The very thought made Gainesmil blanch. He suppressed the images and concentrated instead on Victoria. In the breeze of the open doors, her white linen gown seemed one with the long, flowing curtains. Gainesmil could imagine that she stood naked among the billowing draperies, with the sea air caressing her pale body—he *did* imagine it, in fact, much to his annoyance.

"You didn't answer my question," he said crossly.

But if she heard him, she gave no indication and continued merely to gaze over the harbor. Gainesmil resolved to wait her out. He refused to nip at her heels like some yapping dog. If she didn't value his contributions, then he would leave her to her own devices soon enough, and the loss would be hers.

As he waited, Gainesmil noticed a round locket on a chain lying on the coffee table before him. He remembered having seen Victoria wear the locket at the conference; he could picture how it had lain on her chest...he shook away that image as well. Gainesmil leaned forward in his seat. *It's large enough to have something inside*, he thought, inspecting the sparkling piece of jewelry from the short distance. Victoria might have forgotten his presence, as little notice as she paid him. Slowly, Gainesmil reached toward the golden locket.

"I saw Vitel this very evening," Victoria said. Gainesmil jerked back his hand so quickly that he cracked his elbow on the end table at his side. Tingling pain shot up his arm, but he managed to steady the lamp, which had begun to totter dangerously.

"Vitel seems very..." She turned away from the open doors but still didn't look at Gainesmil. Her chin was raised, as she stared at some indeterminate midpoint and pondered the issue. "Sad. Very sad." Now her gaze locked onto the other Toreador. "Did you feel his loss, Robert?"

Gainesmil lost himself in her sorrowful green eyes. He couldn't quite follow her train of thought but didn't want to admit as much. "I...yes, I...suppose he was sad."

"He lost a childe in the attack on Washington," Victoria explained with barely suppressed emotion. She closed the French doors. "He doesn't know the fate of his other childe. Have you ever Embraced, Robert?" Again her eyes held him.

Gainesmil wetted his lips. "No, I...no."

"The prince has childer, no?"

"Prince Garlotte? Oh, yes." Gainesmil emerged from his confusion as the conversation returned to familiar ground. "You've met Isaac...." He faltered slightly as the image of the bloody, truncated fingers assaulted him again.

"The sheriff."

"Yes," Gainesmil nodded, "the sheriff. The prince has two other childer. Neither show much interest in Kindred affairs. Katrina is a beautiful girl, though she has a bit of a mouth. He dotes on her so." Gainesmil shook his head disapprovingly. "Anyone else who defied him the way she does, he'd have put down long ago."

Victoria slowly crossed to the fireplace and turned off the gas. The flames died away. "Defied him? How so?"

"Oh, however she can think to." Gainesmil rolled his eyes. "Not too long ago she Embraced two mortals without his permission—not one, mind you, but *two*."

"And he took no action?" Victoria sounded unconvinced.

"Brushed it under the rug," Gainesmil explained. "Never has come up as an official matter, though everyone knows.

"Now, Fin, the third, is quite another story, but just as disappointing," he continued. "Can't seem to leave the mortals behind. Has some little wench...er, girl...whom he's mad about."

Victoria took a seat on the end of the couch closest to Gainesmil. She placed a finger on his knee. "Vitel told me something very interesting," she said, abruptly changing subject.

"What was that?" Gainesmil tried to keep up with her, but there were her eyes so close, and her finger tracing circles on his knee.

"He said that the Tremere didn't raise a finger to save Washington."

Gainesmil nodded agreement. "Yes, we've confirmed that from several sources. No thanks to Ms. Chin. It seems that Dorfman, Peter Dorfman, the Pontifex, was out of town, out of the country, in fact, and his underlings felt it more important to protect the chantry than to protect the city."

"And now the Tremere chantry is the only vestige of Camarilla power in Washington," said Victoria. "They should be castigated for such cowardice."

"Or praised," Gainesmil offered, and was satisfied by Victoria's apparent confusion. "Oh yes, that's how they'll play it. How much worse off we'd be without a toehold of any sort from which to retake the city."

"But the city might never have been lost!" Victoria protested.

"Ah, but who among us can testify that the strength within the chantry, if scattered, would have been sufficient to reverse the Sabbat onslaught?" Gainesmil asked, playing devil's advocate.

Victoria understood and continued his line of reasoning: "And the chantry is more valuable as a defensive post, and as a hindrance to the Sabbat's lines of supply and communication should they continue to advance." Victoria nodded. She squeezed Gainesmil's leg and rose from her seat. "Those devils. I will have to speak with Ms. Chin. How long before the next conference?"

Gainesmil glanced at his watch. "Tonight is the eighth. We gather again on the sixteenth, or rather midnight the seventeenth."

Victoria stood above him and placed a long, thin finger over her lips. "And the news from the justicars...?"

Gainesmil shook his head. "Nothing, as far as I know. Prince Garlotte petitioned Justicar Lucinde, but we've heard nothing in way of reply. Those European elders—time is different for many of them."

"Well, I suppose," said Victoria, "they're not in danger of watching their own domains disappear before their wizened old eyes."

"Speaking of disappearing," Gainesmil remembered one of

the reasons for his visit tonight, "there's the matter of a certain employee of the inn—a bellboy?"

Victoria cringed and smiled sheepishly. Gainesmil thought he might even have seen a hint of blush. "They do call it room service...."

Gainesmil sighed. "Please try to control your impulses, Victoria. The staff are only to be used in dire emergencies. Otherwise, with the number of guests in town, we'll be waiting on ourselves."

"Now, we can't have that, can we? I'll control my impulses, Robert," she said, running her fingers through his hair, "if you control yours."

Gainesmil's mouth went dry. Victoria walked past him and opened the double doors to the bedroom. The flick of a switch extinguished all the lights, except for those outside around the harbor. She turned another switch, which began the closing of the specially installed blinds that would block out any exterior light.

"Why doesn't the prince come visit, Robert? I've barely seen him this past week. Has he grown tired of me?" Victoria leaned with her back against the doorway.

As the blinds gradually closed out the last of the light, Gainesmil's eyes adjusted to the increasing darkness. His tongue felt thick as a brick. "I...certainly not...uh, the prince, that is...he's been incredibly busy with the defense of the city, the...uh, stream of refugees has not abated, despite the Sabbat's seeming inertia...."

"I see," Victoria said wistfully. "I'm just not that high among his priorities."

Gainesmil was unable to turn away as she sauntered through the darkness to the bed in the adjacent room. With barely any motion at all, she slipped out of her gown and, naked, beneath the sheets.

"I miss him so," Victoria sighed. "And Robert, do let yourself out."

As if in a stupor, Gainesmil rose and went to the door—the other door, the exit. Not until it was closed behind him did he manage to swallow the lump in his throat.

Monday, 12 July 1999, 12:01 AM (local time)
Executive suite, The International, Ltd.
Amsterdam, The Netherlands

Jan Pieterzoon leaned far back in the overstuffed chair and massaged away the tiny red marks on his nose from the wire-rimmed glasses that now rested on his desk. He craved whiskey. *Needed* whiskey. But it never settled well these nights. He suspected that his stomach had atrophied and shrunken to nothing from the years of disuse. There were, of course, many such stories among the Kindred, but who knew which were mere flights of fancy and which to believe? And to ask an older, more knowledgeable Cainite would be too great an admission of ignorance. For ignorance was weakness, and the weak seldom survived. Not for long.

"Are you all right, Mr. Pieterzoon?"

Jan nodded but neither spoke nor opened his eyes. Marja would still be concerned. She would ask him what she could do for him, and at this moment, the question itself would be enough. Hearing her speak Dutch soothed his nerves. So many of his business contacts were in French, or German, or—God help him—English.

"Can I do anything for you, sir?"

"No thank you, Ms. van Havermaete."

Mr. *Pieterzoon.* Ms. *van Havermaete.* Jan allowed the pained smile slowly to spread across his lips. *How long have you served me, Marja?* Still, the formality. And so it would remain. Jan could not allow himself familiarity between them, and as long as he could not, she would not.

He ran his fingers through his short, blond hair, and then

rubbed the muscles of his ever-smooth jaw. Each muscle in his entire body seemed to be a reservoir of tension, and unfortunately he had no time to seek out his acupuncturist.

"We leave for the United States very soon," Jan said, opening his eyes.

This was news to Marja. "The States? *How* soon?"

"As soon as possible. Within a few nights."

He watched as she digested the information, made lists of the necessary arrangements in her mind. "Business?" she asked.

"Not technically speaking, no."

She nodded. That would impose another set of criteria on her preparations. A trip to meet investors or deal with labor representatives would have been entirely within her realm of operation. If the trip were related, however, to the shadowy dealings of the Kindred, of which she knew only and exactly what she needed to know, other considerations took precedence.

"Security?"

Jan thought for a moment. "Ton and Herman."

"Assistants for yourself?"

"Yourself and Roel." Roel was capable, personable, a good companion for Marja. Jan chose him for that reason. Neither had the slightest idea of the underlying commonality that tied them to Jan.

"That should do. We can augment personnel later, if necessary," Jan explained briefly. "I don't want to waltz in with a full-fledged entourage. Matters may be...sensitive enough without the perception of presumption."

Marja made her mental notes. "Destination?"

"Baltimore. We'll be staying at the Lord Baltimore Inn as guests of Alexander Garlotte. Please make the necessary arrangements," he told her more from habit than from need.

Marja turned to leave the office. Her skirt, longer than was the current style, hung almost to her knees. Her simple yet attractive sweater gave Jan the impression of unintentional seductiveness—or would have if he'd gone in for that sort of thing anymore. *Ironic,* he thought. *I sought a victim and found a trusted associate.*

"Ms. Havermaete," he called just before the door closed. She stepped back into the office. "The factory in Bonn—it will have to be closed. There won't be time to deal with it properly now."

"That's sixteen hundred workers' jobs, sir."

"I'm quite aware of that," Jan responded matter-of-factly. "There are also the financial interests of sixteen investors. The scales are hardly balanced. See that the paperwork goes out in the morning."

"Yes, sir." Then she left him.

Jan did not begrudge Marja her humanitarian impulses. Several of his corporations were ardent supporters of nonprofit organizations. That was how he'd found her in the first place. His own philanthropic tendencies might be more focused, but they were no less sincere for that. It was one of his few concessions to conscience.

As Marja's footsteps receded beyond the door, Jan reluctantly turned his thoughts back to the events that had necessitated his upcoming journey.

"Our friends across the Atlantic seem unable to deal with their difficulties," Hardestadt had said. Jan had made the trip down to Nantes, to one of Hardestadt's countless havens, at the behest of the elder Ventrue. Such a personal audience was not typical. "You are aware of the Sabbat disruptions on the North American continent?" Hardestadt asked as he passed a silver goblet to Jan across the small space between their matching Louis Quinze chairs.

"Yes, my sire." Jan felt so small next to the man. A backdrop of centuries lent additional stature to the elder's strong chin and aristocratic features. The study in which they sat, despite the plush rug, the velvet curtains, and the inviting grain of the mahogany bookshelves, was cold. Sterile. Unchanging. As he raised the goblet to his lips, the mere bouquet of the vitae set Jan's head swimming. Just a sip—the life's blood of elders long ago sent to Final Death—burned his mouth and throat, but the burning danced maddeningly along the thin line between pain and pleasure. Warmth spread throughout Jan's torso, his arms and legs. He felt color rising to his usually colorless face.

"You will have to go over there and straighten out this mess," said Hardestadt.

Jan, dizzy after his second sip from the goblet, thought he must have heard incorrectly. There was much honor to be gained in such an affair, but certain niggling details demanded his increasingly fogged attention. "I am to accompany the military command?" he inquired.

"You *are* the command," Hardestadt said bluntly. "Events elsewhere do not allow us to expend unlimited resources in assisting our cousins. The Sabbat are delinquent malcontents, have been from the beginning. Return them to their place. And try not to be too long about it."

The significance of the words, the immensity of the task, slowly permeated Jan's reeling mind. Open warfare raged in the streets of America. The Sabbat had somehow achieved a coordination of action at a level that had eluded them for the centuries since their inception. It was a situation worthy of the attentions of a justicar, of a whole *band* of justicars. And Jan was being sent to take care of the matter. By himself.

"Yes, my sire."

Jan took a large draught from the goblet, as large as politely possible. The fire cleansed him from within.

"I know you will not fail me in this," Hardestadt said.

I will not fail you, Jan silently nodded agreement. *I will not fail you…and survive.*

Monday, 12 July 1999, 11:05 PM
Exit 33, Interstate 95
Laurel, Maryland

"There have always been devotees to hedonism, people living only for the pleasure of the moment," Christof said with his slight French accent, "but now there are *so many*."

"Now as opposed to when?" Lydia asked.

"As opposed to..." Christof suddenly seemed almost to forget their conversation, to become lost in his own thoughts. His relaxed, easy manner shifted almost instantly to brooding melancholy. "...To before. Long ago."

As Lydia guided the car to the exit lane, she glanced over at her passenger. It wasn't just his accent and mane of blazing red hair that made him stand out from the typical Brujah, she decided. The majority of her clanmates were fratboy-biker-excon-rolled-into-one types. To them, *revolution* was code for *tear up what's there now, and we'll figure out something better later.* Christof was one of the few with a more philosophical bent. He seemed to have a better idea of where he wanted to be going.

Must have something to do with that chick he's always talking about, Lydia thought; though to be fair, he wasn't *always* talking about her. In fact, it had been like pulling fangs to get him to say *anything* about her, and still all Lydia knew was that the girl's name was Anezka, or something goofy like that, and that Christof was looking for her. Lydia's pondering was interrupted by a commotion from her other passengers in the back seat.

"Hey, why you gettin' off here?" Frankie asked.

"Yeah," chimed in Baldur. "We ain't to D.C. yet.

You want to pee gas into the tank?" Lydia asked. "And we're

not going all the way into D.C." Not *with you assholes*, she thought. *And not without Theo.*

Probably they wouldn't go much past the Beltway. This was just a reconnaissance, not an assault. Besides, with the curfew in Washington proper, a lot of the restless Sabbat types had migrated northeast of the city. This stretch of road was dangerous enough without her trying to win the war backed up by only one philosopher, Tweedledumb, and Tweedledipshit.

"Hey Frankie," said Baldur, apparently satisfied with Lydia's answer and getting back to the important business of tormenting his companion, "wanna go to Hollywood?"

"Hey! At least I didn't name myself after a damn computer game."

"You can't even *spell* computer. Not my fault if you peaked with Space Invaders. Or was it Pong?"

"How'd you like my foot up *your* gate?"

Lydia sighed. Christof didn't seem inclined toward more conversation—sure, he was philosophical, but he was also fucking moody as a girl—so she turned up the radio in an effort to drown out the mindless drivel from the backseat. She turned off the exit ramp and into the first gas station, which was doing a brisk business. The others stayed in the car while she pumped. Freed for the moment from having to think about asshole drivers on the interstate, not to mention the assholes in the backseat of her own car, Lydia's mind turned again to Theo Bell.

The archon, in many ways was her exact opposite—tall, dark, and massive to her small, pale, and skinny—but Lydia liked to think that they thought similarly. That wasn't to say that she didn't have a lot to learn from him, because she did. About tactics, about patience, about getting people to do what she wanted them to do. Of course, Theo had an advantage in that last department, being a life-size Mt. Rushmore, but beyond sheer intimidation, he knew how to read people. And he knew that the more you ordered folks around, the less they listened.

That night at the conference, when the news had first broken that the Sabbat was in Washington, Lydia would have been tempted to collar the Anarch horde before they ran off for a slugfest in the streets. That wasn't a game the Camarilla could win. But Theo had let them go. He'd sat and not said a word as the younger Brujah had hightailed it south. They'd gotten their butts kicked. A few of them never came back. But most of them did, and by then they'd gotten that big adrenaline rush out of their systems and were ready to listen to Theo.

Since then, things had gone relatively smoothly. Theo had set up reconnaissance patrols along with the occasional raid south to gauge the Sabbat's strength and organization. The area between D.C. and Baltimore was still pretty much a no-man's-land, but if the Sabbat was preparing to come north in force, Theo would know.

As the gas pump whirred off the dollars and gallons, Lydia turned and found herself staring at the guy on the other side of the island who was filling up an old, beat-up Buick. It took several seconds to sink in, what had caught her attention: his unnaturally pale complexion, his drawn skin and almost skeletal profile.

Vampire? she wondered. She couldn't tell, but she did know that if he *was* Kindred, he wasn't one of theirs.

Just then, he turned and saw Lydia. For a long moment, they both stood there, not fifteen feet apart, staring at one another as the same realization sank in on both sides of the pump. Then he hissed.

He reached under his shirt, but Lydia was already in the air. Her steel toe-capped boot caught him in the face, and they both landed hard on the cement. Lydia rolled clear and took cover behind another car. She thought she'd seen other people in the Buick, and they might come up shooting.

"Christof! Frankie!" she yelled. She could hear car doors opening.

"Pop the trunk, Bubby," said somebody who sounded like he was holding a broken jaw.

Fuck this, Lydia decided. She grabbed the .38 from her pocket and jumped to her feet firing. The Buick's back window shattered. A second later, Christof's booming, long-barreled .44 joined the fray. Frankie and Baldur were right with him. Each had a 9mm, put to good use. The Buick rocked as the bullets struck home. Glass sprayed in every direction. Customers were screaming, running, throwing themselves behind cover.

But somebody inside the Buick had reached the lever for the trunk. It popped open...and the *thing* unfolded itself from inside.

Its head and torso were vaguely human, but as it stepped free of the car, its lower half resembled a five-legged spider. Long, jointed legs stretched out until it stood nearly eight feet tall. It scuttled straight for Lydia.

She fired her last two bullets into its chest. It didn't even slow down. Lydia reached into her pocket for more bullets, but the metal casings slipped through her suddenly clumsy fingers. She couldn't take her eyes from the charging monstrosity, not until one of its legs caught her across the chest. Suddenly she was airborne. She crashed to the pavement on her face, felt her nose crushed, skin scraped away. She tasted blood. Her hands were empty, the .38 gone.

Lydia looked up at the spider-thing above her—how could it move so quickly?—but she was too dazed to roll out of the way.

The flash of steel blinded her—that and the spray of blood across her face. The spider shuddered and bellowed in pain. Another flash. More blood.

Lydia made herself roll away from the monster. Christof was there. Instead of his .44, he was wielding his sword—the sword she had teased him for carrying around under his duster.

Then Lydia was wiping her hands across her face and licking the blood from them. She should help Christof, but he seemed to have things under control. And she couldn't help herself. There was so much blood. She was covered in it.

The bullet ripping into her leg got her attention. Christof might have dispatched the spider-thing, but there was still the small matter of Sabbat vampires. In fact, the sounds of combat had apparently gotten the attention of several other carloads of the fuckers on the other side of the gas station.

Someone nearby gunned an engine. A car—*her* car—was coming right for Lydia. It swerved and screeched to a stop right by her.

"Let's go!" Frankie was behind the wheel. He barely waited for Lydia and Christof to jump in before peeling away.

"Get on the phone!" Lydia yelled. "Get Theo!"

Monday, 12 July 1999, 11:43 PM
The Sunken Cathedral
CranberryBogs, Massachusetts

From the moment he had first fallen into the hands of the Nosferatu, Benito Giovanni had fully expected to be tortured. He had been resigned to it, prepared for it. Almost, he was looking forward to it. Not out of some perverse titillation, but rather in the same way he hung upon the handshake that sealed a tricky business deal. It was the serenity of closure he longed for—in this case, an end to the years of secrecy and anxiety.

They had snatched him from his penthouse office, his private sanctum, the very pinnacle of his worldly power.

His influence—the influence of the Giovanni family—overshadowed the city of Boston. It was *their* city. The Giovanni had held it against the advances of both the Camarilla and the Sabbat. The mayor, the police commissioner, the captains of industry, the archbishop, the old-money families—all of these powers could be summoned to Benito's aid at the tap of his speed-dial. He had been enthroned at the very center of the intricate web of connections and manipulations that made up the subtle framework of his domain.

And the Nosferatu had walked right in and taken him.

They would torture him, that much was certain. And he, in turn, would tell them everything he knew about this whole unpleasant business.

Unfortunately, Benito admitted, the sum of all he knew about this deal still amounted to very little. Too little, he feared, to satisfy a determined Inquisitor.

He had arranged the commission, of course. But he was

just the deal broker, the matchmaker. It was no great secret in Kindred circles that Benito Giovanni's connections in the art world were extensive. He had something of a reputation for conjuring up masterpieces that were widely held to be lost to the depredations of time and political upheaval. This reputation was due, in no small part, to Benito's crusade in the years following the close of World War II to quietly liberate many priceless works of art that had been plundered by the Reich. A steady stream of these treasures found their way to Boston and from there into the hands of a very select clientele of museums and private collectors.

Among the Toreador clan, with their almost religious devotion to the arts, Benito was romantically viewed as something of a cross between a saint and a rumrunner. If the truth were known, Benito found this tribute more than a bit embarrassing. He went to great lengths, however, to cultivate and maintain the goodwill of the Toreador. Although individually, *les Artistes* could be fickle and capricious, their knowledge and contacts were a peerless competitive advantage in his line of work.

One of the many benefits of his de facto partnership with the Toreador was the unending stream of invitations to the great fetes, balls and galas with which *les Artistes* marked the unending progression of the seasons. These decadent outlets for their ennui provided Benito with unrivaled opportunities to come into contact with the real powerbrokers—the princes and primogen of the major cities on both sides of the Atlantic.

Benito allowed himself a muttered curse as he tried to check his watch. It had been confiscated, of course, at the time of his abduction. This was perhaps the thousandth time he had caught himself in the middle of this little ritual. He had been thinking about missed appointments, about the Summer Solstice party that Victoria Ash had given in Atlanta. It was long over by now.

Missed opportunities.

Victoria was an up-and-comer, someone to watch in the nights ahead. She had only recently relocated to Atlanta in a bold play for a recently vacated spot on the city's primogen council. The Solstice gathering was something of a coming-out party for her—the opening volley in her bid for the big time.

As valuable a contact as Victoria was, however, she was not the sole attraction of the Solstice party. She had given him to believe that not only would the mad Prince Benison of Atlanta be present (which might be expected), but also that Julius, the Brujah archon, would be making a special appearance. This volatile combination threatened to explode dramatically, raining down shards of power, prestige and influence upon those bold enough to grab them. Benito keenly regretted not being on hand for the fireworks, but the phone call and that voice—that damnable voice that he'd hoped never to hear again—had necessitated that Benito cancel.

How ironic, that he'd again been assaulted by that voice and then fallen victim to these captors. Ironic, but certainly not coincidental.

His captors, the Nosferatu, had a reputation for extracting secrets. Benito had no illusions about playing the hero, about spitting in the face of his Inquisitor. They would learn all, of course, in due time.

And still, they would demand to know more. Knowledge was a compulsion for them, an addiction. They would press him ever more closely, driving home their pointed inquires with fire and the stake. He would shamelessly blubber forth all he knew. Then he would progress to further details conjured from pure fancy and desperation.

Still they would pry deeper.

Benito had one hope, and that a feeble one. He would give them everything they asked for. He would ration it out over a gratifyingly long period of time, long enough that they might be convinced of the veracity of his confessions—or at least the veracity of their instruments of extracting confessions. He would then throw himself on their mercy and beg the deformed, the hideous, the grotesque outcasts to have pity upon his poor broken body and suffer him to live.

It did not seem a likely thing to hope for, but it was all he had.

To maintain this fleeting and ephemeral hope, Benito first had to convince himself that, above all, the Nosferatu were true devotees of knowledge. If he could only bring himself to believe that their highest—in fact, their only—concern in this matter was learning the truth, then all was not lost. Once they had discovered the role that Benito had played in this matter—and that he was blameless of the blood spilled—they would release him.

The one nagging doubt that threatened to collapse this fanciful construct was that he was not entirely convinced the Nosferatu paid more than passing lip service to the altar of Knowledge. Deep down, he harbored a tenacious suspicion that their idol was, conversely, the stunted god of Secrets.

Secrets, a very specialized form of knowledge—the power of which was diminished by the number of people who possessed them.

Once Benito shared his knowledge of these events with his Inquisitor, the true power of the revelation would be diluted, diminished by half. The only way to restore the secret to its full potency would be to eliminate one of its keepers. It was not difficult to calculate the exact probability of Benito's surviving an encounter with the cult of secrecy.

Benito was prepared for hot irons and wicked knives and barbed stakes. What he was not prepared for was the maddeningly steady advance of the canonical hours.

The bell was tolling the office. Matins, he imagined, although it was difficult to say with any certainty. The muffled footfalls of countless comings and goings never seemed to slow, much less cease. But surely even the Nosferatu, bred to endless generations of subterranean existence, must still be subject to the primeval progression of day and night.

The bells were only the primary player in the complex tapestry of sound that filled his captivity. At times he heard whispers from beyond the confines of his ascetic cell. At other times, chanting. At other times still, the sharp scratch of pen on parchment.

But at no time did he hear the sound he most expected: the turning of a key in the lock. The unmistakable sign that he was, at last, in the presence of his Inquisitor.

Entire nights, weeks, had passed, if the tolling of the bells was to be believed. Thus far, he had yet even to catch a glimpse of his circumspect captors. Benito, suspicious by nature, was not yet willing to rule out the possibility that the tolling of the hours might itself be a subtle form of torture—a way for his captors to play with his perceptions, to muddle his sense of time, to fuel his desperation. The cumulative message of the bells was clear enough. If his trail were already several weeks cold, Benito could have little hope of outside assistance, of rescue by his family or their many agents. With each clanging of the bells, it became more obvious that Benito was utterly alone, cut off from his resources and totally at the mercy of his captors.

The church bells had an additional effect of which his abductors certainly could not be ignorant. The holy clamor tended to ward off any possible intervention by allies from beyond the Pale. Benito had tried several times to reach out through the pathways of spirit to make contact, to send a message, to summon aid. But to no avail. The denizens of the spirit realm gave this sacred ground—though fallen into ruin and disuse many generations past—a wide berth.

With each passing night, the anxiety, the desperation and the hunger grew. Benito counted out the period of his captivity in missed appointments and lost opportunities.

And all the while, the Beast grew bolder, gnawing away at reason and straining at its tether.

Monday, 12 July 1999, 11:49 PM
Main lobby, Lord Baltimore Inn
Baltimore, Maryland

"May I get anything else for you, ma'am?" Victoria raised the glass of rich, red wine and wet her lips, then deigned to acknowledge the costumed young man. "Not at the moment, thank you." He bowed and backed away, as pleased as if she'd handed him a hundred-dollar tip. Victoria, ensconced in the padded armchair in the lobby of the Lord Baltimore, was holding court, of sorts, as various of the inn employees saw to her every need.

What's the point of having mortals around, she wondered, *if they're not performing the menial little tasks that make them feel so useful?* It was a situation that left everyone rewarded, not the least of all Victoria. She was in her element with others fawning over her, and it was a pleasant and innocent enough diversion from how she'd been spending most of her time the past nights— gathering information, and none of it too awfully helpful.

The flow of refugees into the city had now slowed to a trickle, two and a half weeks after the Sabbat had rolled into Washington, three weeks since her sabotaged social gala in Atlanta. And it must have been sabotaged. Of that, she was certain. And at least two other ideas were certainties in her mind: first, that she would discover who was responsible for her betrayal; second, that they would pay.

The primary suspects seemed to be Rolph, the Nosferatu sewer rat she'd invited out of the goodness of her heart, and Erich Vegel, the Setite antiquarian whom Victoria had toyed with to such effect. Each had seemed to be missing shortly before the Sabbat attack fell, neither having taken proper leave by informing the hostess. Rolph's disappearance was not necessarily sinister. The Nosferatu were always skulking around on the fringes of respectable Kindred society and, truth be told, Victoria might have just missed him while he was still there. Vegel's case was the more perplexing, for it was a call from his master that had alerted Victoria to her guest's absence—*if* it really had been Hesha on the other end of that conversation, and *if* the call itself was not a ruse to suggest that Vegel's exit was spontaneous. Possible. A scheme within a scheme. But then the Setites who had inadvertently rescued Victoria from Atlanta had been seeking Vegel. That seemed to imply that he was in trouble as well. *Unless* the rescue, like the phone call, had been orchestrated to impart to Victoria exactly that impression! Could Hesha be so wily? Or could Vegel have gone rogue—if that was possible for a Setite—and given both Victoria and his erstwhile employer the slip?

Her investigations into these matters had gone...well, nowhere. Mainly because, as of yet, she had encountered no other survivors from Atlanta. None. From Gainesmil, eternal font of information that he was, she'd learned that Hesha actually kept residence in Baltimore—a situation to which Prince Garlotte had not completely resolved himself. But so long as the Setite kept a low profile, the cost of a full-fledged snake hunt seemed prohibitive.

There was also Benito Giovanni, who at the last moment had cancelled his trip to Atlanta for the party. Could he have known something about the Sabbat attack? Victoria would never rule out the possibility of a member of the treacherous Giovanni clan colluding with the Sabbat, but finding out anything about the tight-knit clan was next to impossible. She had heard rumors—through Gainesmil, again—that Benito had disappeared sometime around the party. With the Giovanni, however, who knew what that might really mean?

Otherwise, Victoria had busied herself in meeting many of the refugees. On the whole, they were touchingly grateful, but Victoria felt certain that if she had to empathize with anyone else within the next, say, ten years, she would throw up. The masses would provide some support for her at the next conference, only four nights away, but the key players, the individuals who would determine the outcome of events, lingered beyond her control.

Once the flow of refugees had begun to slow, Prince Garlotte had visited her more frequently. Victoria raised a hand to her neck, slid her fingers along the chain to the locket that was never far from her. The prince seemed to take pleasure in seeing her wear the piece. Victoria, in her own way, took comfort from the soft metal resting near her heart. Despite Garlotte's obvious affection for her, however, the prince remained wary. Victoria didn't expect him to turn over his city to her—not that she would quibble if he did—but she did hope for more forthright support from him in public gatherings. If that support did not materialize, and soon, she might be forced to take stern measures. For now, though, he actively sought her company; he considered himself strong enough to resist her selectively, and perhaps he was. For now.

Gainesmil, on the other hand, was a clay pigeon that Victoria could pluck from the air whenever she pleased. She left him enough free will that he could imagine he was independent, and watched with amusement his noble struggle of conscience between his loyalties to his prince and to his clanmate. Victoria knew there was less of conscience and more of weather vane to his moral dilemma. Whichever way the wind blew, there would be Gainesmil.

The Malkavians, as usual, were irrelevant. Aside from Prince Benison of Atlanta, she'd never met a member of that clan who was worth a thimbleful of vitae.

She'd had no opportunity to speak with Theo Bell and suspected that he would not accept her invitation to a tête-à-tête, even if occasion did arise—which was not likely to happen. The brute had stayed busy with his rabble patrolling the stretch of real estate between Washington and Baltimore, and had even gone so far as to lead minor incursions into the hostile capital. *Good for him*, Victoria thought. His was the type of dedication that would keep her safe, and rightly so. Additionally, he seemed to be one of a rare breed of Brujah—those who know their place.

Marcus Vitel, prince of that other city, *former* prince—Victoria saw little hope of wresting the city from the Sabbat, despite all Brujah zeal—seemed to be in mourning, for his city or for his childer, Victoria didn't know. Rumor had it (and Gainesmil confirmed) that Vitel was responsible, at least in part, for the martial law that had been imposed in Washington and made more difficult the Sabbat's consolidation of control in the city.

Vitel had taken up residence in a private townhouse, and though he had not turned away Victoria's visits over the past two weeks, neither had he proven particularly talkative. Still, she had begun the process of feeling him out, of determining what it was that would open his inner desires to her. Perhaps it was sympathy for his poor childer that would hook him.

Dear God, Victoria thought. *More sympathy.*

For all practical purposes, that left only Maria Chin, the representative of the Tremere. Victoria felt the knowledge that the Tremere in Washington, Chin's own chantry, had watched idly as the city had fallen to the Sabbat might be of some use. Perhaps there was a deal to be made. Victoria could defend the actions of the Tremere in return for the clan's support in the conference. There was, of course, the complicating factor that the Tremere might, as Gainesmil and later Vitel had suggested, simply take the position that they were more concerned with the long-term interests of the Camarilla—maintaining the sect's presence in D.C.—than in propping up a Ventrue prince in the short term. The Tremere might not need Victoria's defense. But surely, she hoped, they would see the benefit of having friends in the conference, and there was no harm in attempting to lay the groundwork for mutual support in the future.

That was why Victoria had ventured down to the lobby of the Lord Baltimore Inn in the first place. Chin had agreed to come speak with her. Victoria glanced at her diamond-studded watch and was completely unsurprised to see Chin walk through the lobby doors precisely at midnight, exactly on time. Victoria rose to greet her visitor, and completely ignored the mortal employees of the inn who scurried away in every direction, each fearful that he or she had somehow offended the elegant guest and was personally responsible for her departure.

"Maria," said Victoria, taking a friendly, familiar tone.

The Tremere's expression remained unchanged, neutral. "Ms. Ash." She wore a long gray-blue robe with the hood back. It struck Victoria as slightly anachronistic, but that was hardly a sin or even out of the ordinary with Kindred.

Victoria took her guest by the arm and led her toward the elevator. "I took it upon myself to wait for you personally— how very gauche, I know—but I'm afraid none of my servants made the trip north with me, and there's just been no time for interviews…" Victoria kept up the patter, quite innocuous talk to any mortal who might be within earshot. Chin did not contribute to the conversation or attempt to address Victoria's rhetorical questions.

Bubbling over with personality, this one, Victoria thought wryly, but wasn't that the case with all Tremere? As she turned her key to send them on their way to the seventh floor, the Toreador was tempted to seduce Maria right then and there, just to see some type of reaction from the woman. *I could do it before we reached the fifth floor,* Victoria thought, but decided against it. There was little sense in jeopardizing future gains for such petty gratification at this point.

What actually did happen before they reached the fifth floor was quite different. Victoria was chatting away, making up for the silence of her companion. Neither occupant of the elevator saw or heard the hatch open in the ceiling, or the speciallycrafted garrote that lowered through the portal. Not until Maria Chin's feet were dangling two feet above the floor did Victoria realize something was wrong, and even then it took a moment for the sight of the Tremere's bulging eyes and flailing arms to sink in.

Victoria saw the hands, the black gloves, pulling forcefully on the wire behind Maria's neck. Immediately, Victoria's instincts for dealing with danger took over—she screamed bloody murder.

It seemed to her that her scream provided the impetus for the wire as it sliced upward under Chin's jaw. Victoria was pressed back against the corner, her mouth still open wide, when the garrote completely separated skull from spine, and both portions of Maria Chin thudded to the floor.

part two:

domain

Saturday, 17 July 1999, 12:37 AM
McHenry Auditorium, Lord Baltimore Inn
Baltimore, Maryland

Security was heavy. Not surprising considering the events of just a few nights past. Jan slipped in as unobtrusively as possible through the door near the head of the auditorium and occupied a vacant seat on the front row. En route, he nodded a polite greeting to Prince Garlotte, who stood near the center of the well. At the moment, however, Victoria Ash seemed to have the floor and was speaking to the receptive gathering.

Jan had known that Victoria would be present, yet the first sight of her triggered a slight fibrillation in his chest. He had first met her years ago at a social event in Paris, then seen her again on similar occasions in London and New York. He'd seen her last three years ago; she'd attended one of his corporate galas in Amsterdam. Each of the encounters had been brief, polite, consisting mostly of superficial pleasantries, yet each time, he'd walked away feeling the exchange had been…loaded, that each word brimmed with meaning and passion revealed only in tiny, innocuous, *maddening* morsels. There was no single phrase or glance on which he could pin this feeling, yet the impression persisted, and was renewed more forcefully with their every meeting.

Tonight was no exception. Victoria wore an off-white, beaded gown. The high neck was conservative, but the dress was form-fitting and complimented her figure nicely. Her long gloves and the gold locket that hung from her neck lent an air of stateliness, while the plunging lines of the dress's back teased of the sensual. Jan's initial reaction was the desire to lead her from this crowded chamber and sit with her privately, to spend hours doing nothing but listening to the music of her voice and gazing upon her beauty.

Jan closed his eyes tightly and squeezed the bridge of his nose, a gesture born only partly of fatigue. He struggled to clear his mind. From his brief conversation with Prince Garlotte earlier, and from what he'd learned from other sources, Victoria was likely to be, if anything, an impediment to the task at hand. Jan could not afford to allow gentle feelings to stand in his way. Regardless, he knew quite well that his attraction to her was the result of more than her charming personality and pleasing appearance. More subtle forces were at work, and to be enthralled by one such as her would not be wise. That knowledge, however, did little to diminish the allure of the prospect.

"Baltimore must become the bastion of Camarilla resistance," Victoria was saying. Murmurs of agreement rose from the assembly. "This city will become the bulwark against which the fiends of the Sabbat cannot hope to prevail, and then we shall turn the tide. How else will we ever regain Charleston, Abigail? Or Richmond, Peter?" The individuals mentioned, and others, nodded solemnly and voiced their support.

Jan casually surveyed the chamber. Theo Bell appeared to be among the unconvinced. He sat, arms crossed, silent as the sphinx. Judging by appearances—not always accurate, Jan knew—there seemed to be a sprinkling of other Brujah seated around the brooding archon, though not as many and not as boisterous as reported from the first meeting of the conference. Jan suspected that their numbers and their enthusiasm had been thinned somewhat by the vigorous resistance Bell had been coordinating on the outskirts of Washington.

There was Robert Gainesmil, Prince Garlotte's Toreador advisor, and not far from him another figure of decidedly noble bearing. Jan had never met Marcus Vitel in person, but knew of the prince of Washington, D.C., enough to recognize him on sight. The exiled prince seemed practically disinterested in Victoria's platitudes. He watched through eyes of the defeated. While Victoria had been driven from a city, Vitel had been driven from *his* city. He was more intimately familiar with the odds they faced.

Another face of skepticism among the malleable crowd was that of the Tremere representative, Aisling Sturbridge, regent of the chantry in New York City. She was a slightly built woman who appeared in her mid-thirties by mortal reckoning—as little as that meant among the Kindred. A long, black ponytail hung over the shoulder of her stiff business suit, and an open laptop computer rested on her knees. Jan knew all the gory details relating to the previous Tremere representative to the conference—the assassination to which Victoria had been a witness, an innocent bystander, if her account were given weight. The assassin had, of course, escaped—so utterly without trace that some Kindred were left to speculate about the loyalty of certain Nosferatu, while others spoke in hushed tones of a more menacing possibility. *Clan Assamite.*

As Jan's gaze drifted back to Victoria, he was careful to keep a tight rein on his thoughts. Business must be tended to. Hardestadt would not brook failure.

Without the flagrantly disruptive competition from the Brujah, Victoria seemed to be encountering little resistance in her address to the gathering. The collection of refugees continued to nod and echo her pronouncements on the necessity of concerted effort. As Jan watched, she came to a natural pause and her vibrant, green eyes turned to gaze directly at him. She blinked, slowly, once, and Jan felt a tickle against his cheek, as if her dark eyelashes caressed him across the few yards separating them.

Prince Garlotte stepped forward and drew the attention of the assembly. "Fellow Kindred, allow me to take this opportunity to present an esteemed guest who we are honored to have with us this evening: Mr. Jan Pieterzoon of Amsterdam."

Jan nodded again to the prince and stood, as all eyes in the auditorium turned to him. "Ladies, gentlemen." He bowed to the assemblage.

The prince, whose response to Jan in their brief conversation had been mixed, fell silent, and so the first question seemed naturally to fall to Victoria. "Mr. Pieterzoon," her smile washed over him like a warm bath, "welcome to Baltimore, to the

United States." Her eyes were electric, but Jan held firm and was
not drawn in. "What news do you bring from our European
friends?"

Jan held her gaze momentarily, let her see that he would
stand his ground, then shifted his position so that in facing
her and the prince he did not have his back to the rest of the
gathering. He smiled slightly and looked over the seats. These
were delicate seconds, and Jan would not be rushed. He chose
his words carefully. "I thank Prince Garlotte, and the rest of
you, for your hospitality. It has been several years since I visited
these shores. I only wish that we met under more leisurely
circumstances."

An expectant silence quickly overpowered the minimal
anxious shuffling in the auditorium.

"I am pleased to hear you speaking of concerted action
to turn back the Sabbat, for this is the strategy I am here to
advocate," he said. "These attacks launched by the Sabbat,
beginning in Atlanta just over three weeks ago, are unlike any
we've seen before. They are a greater threat than any we've faced
before." He paused to let his words sink in. Jan was not telling
them anything they did not already know, nor was he trying
to comfort them. He was giving voice to their considerable and
legitimate fears, without resorting to the popular wooing he'd
heard from Victoria.

"I have been sent by the elders of the Camarilla to support
this effort, to lend aid in coordinating the defense," Jan said.

A murmur swept through the gathering. The palpable
anxiety seemed to slacken the least bit, as Jan had intended.

"So you bring with you troops to oppose the Sabbat?"
Victoria asked.

"No," Jan answered quickly. Equivocation at this critical
juncture would be fatal, could only be seen as a sign of weakness.
"The elders, my sire Hardestadt the Elder among them, believe
there are resources enough here to meet the threat."

Total silence. Jan had spoken boldly. Most of what he said he
believed to be true, though the implication that the decision had
come through an organized, deliberative process of the elders
he rather overstated. In truth, he had no idea how the decision

had been reached, or exactly who had been involved. He only knew the scant details that Hardestadt had revealed to him. Now, Jan waited for the inevitable backlash.

Of the American Kindred, Victoria found her voice first. "No? Just...no? You bring no military force whatsoever?"

"That is correct," said Jan without missing a beat. "I bring my personal experience and the support of—"

"Treachery!" someone shouted. Others took up the call.

The Brujah element, subdued until this point, came to their feet as one—except for Bell, whose expression and manner remained unchanged. The others howled in protest. They filled the air with insults and threats directed at Jan and his Old World masters. In one instant, they'd become ardent supporters of Victoria, as Jan knew they must.

The other refugees reacted vehemently to the news as well. Heated and desperate conversations flared around the chamber. One Kindred—a Malkavian, Jan hoped—actually tore hair from his scalp and gave in to tears. Most others reacted less extremely, but none favorably.

Prince Garlotte moved closer to Jan. Jan had given this same news to the prince earlier, so Garlotte, though not pleased, was not surprised. Nor would he have been surprised by the reception Jan received. Garlotte's concern now was for his guest's safety.

"I think you'd better come with me," the prince said, indicating the nearby door through which Jan had entered not long ago.

Jan raised a restraining hand to his clansman, the prince. "I will stay."

Garlotte eyed the increasingly threatening crowd, and nodded respectfully to Jan. The Brujah had resorted to uprooting seats again, one of which flew past not too far from Jan and the prince. Garlotte signaled to Gainesmil, then moved closer to the throng with his hands raised before him. Gainesmil began to circulate among the crowd and speak quietly to those he knew personally. Gradually, and seemingly of its own accord, the din lessened. Soon relative calm was restored.

The disbelief smoldering in Victoria's eyes was representative of those around her. "With all due respect, Mr. Pieterzoon," she said with thinly veiled daggers in her voice, "what use are you to us? How is a lone...*ambassador* going to turn back the Sabbat?"

Jan took on a thoughtful expression. He clasped his hands behind his back and moved away from the door. He walked past Garlotte, past Victoria, and made his way to the center of the well. He ignored the assembled Kindred, perhaps fifty of them, the mob that moments before had threatened to tear him limb from limb, to stake him, to leave him out for the sun, and worse. He ignored them, but felt each one of them watching his deliberate movement. *Let them watch*, he thought.

"No single individual," Jan said, "is going to turn back the Sabbat, Ms. Ash. Not me, not yourself, nor the prince, not even the capable Archon Bell." He gestured toward Theo. "But I may be of some assistance in planning the defense. *Our* defense. For the Camarilla is one body, and should the Sabbat triumph in North America," he paused for what would have been a long breath, "it would be only a matter of time until they triumphed in Europe. The elders are quite aware of that fact, of the necessity of stopping the Sabbat here and now.

"What, may I ask," he said quickly before Victoria could interject a comment, "do you consider to be the purpose of this conference, which I believe you initiated, Ms. Ash?"

Victoria was taken aback by his question, but only momentarily; then she smiled and replied in her polished manner, "I consider this conference to be the entity best able to coordinate the defense of the territory remaining to the Camarilla, and to reclaim that which has been lost."

"And how should it function?" he asked.

Victoria's eyebrow raised. "Meaning...?"

Meaning," Jan said, beginning to take on a scholarly tone, "what specific role should this conference fulfill? There are princes and their advisors in each Camarilla city." He gestured toward Garlotte. "Do they not coordinate their own defenses?"

"Of course, each prince ably defends his own city," Victoria said, "but isolated cities cannot stand against the fury of the Sabbat, against this army of beasts that marches against us."

"Again, I ask, how should this body function? How,

specifically, in relation to the princes? Should they subject themselves to the decisions of your conference?"

"It is not *my* conference," Victoria snapped, somehow without seeming to lose her temper. "And the decisions should flow from this body."

"The princes should subject themselves to the decisions of this conference?"

"Yes," Victoria said. "They should subject themselves to the decisions of this conference—for the good of the many." She swept her hand through the air, indicating the members of the assembly, and again mutterings of support emanated from their number.

Prince Garlotte unwittingly mimicked Theo's manner by crossing his arms.

"The princes already answer to a higher authority," Jan said. "It is called the Camarilla." The mutterings died away. "And the deliberative body of the Camarilla is known as a conclave, the highest of which is the Inner Circle." Jan still spoke to Victoria, but his words were aimed at the broader audience. "Are you, Ms. Ash, a justicar empowered to name this gathering a conclave? Does this body seek to usurp the prerogatives of the Inner Circle in naming you justicar?"

"Of course not!" Victoria answered at once, but then faltered. "I never claimed...no one here..."

"Prince Garlotte petitioned Justicar Lucinde of Clan Ventrue, a duly elected representative of the Camarilla," Jan continued. "I am the duly appointed representative sent by the Camarilla, by the elders of our clans, to assist with the defense and counteroffensive against the Sabbat." Steeled blue eyes locked with fiery green as he held Victoria's gaze. Then Jan turned away from her and to the assembly as a whole. Again, he perhaps overstated the official dimension of his appointment, but who was there here to question him? Who would oppose the will of Hardestadt the Elder, founder of the Camarilla?

"I am not here to subject anyone," Jan said. He looked into the eyes of many of the assembled Kindred, then turned and moved closer to Prince Garlotte. "I am here to extend the hand of partnership to the princes of North America, to help coordinate their efforts. Not to dictate terms to them."

Victoria felt the shift in momentum as much as anyone. "I was not suggesting...of course the princes would have a voice in the conference...."

"I apologize for my tardiness this evening," Jan said, ignoring the protestations of the Toreador. "I was speaking with Prince Michaela of New York. She reports that the situation there is stable, or as stable as it ever is. The effort that has gained our enemies so much in the South is seemingly not replicated in the northern climes. Similar news from Hartford and Buffalo. I spoke with those princes upon my arrival last night."

"But the Sabbat army is before us in Washington," said Gainesmil, taking up the argument on Victoria's behalf. He seemed to have at least one foot firmly in the camp of his fellow Toreador—a detail Prince Garlotte had not mentioned to Jan during the course of their short conversation. "Why *would* there be any trouble in the North?" An approving ripple of comments spread through the auditorium.

"The army to the south facing us is formidable," Jan conceded, "but we would be gravely mistaken to believe that it consisted of every Sabbat on the continent. My sources indicate that some individuals from New York City took part in the attacks, but that otherwise there was practically no involvement from Montreal, Detroit, Pittsburgh, Philadelphia, Portland—"

As he listed the various Sabbat strongholds, many of the Kindred who had assumed they would gather an army and then drive the Sabbat back to the Gulf of Mexico fell into an awed silence as the truly desperate nature of their situation dawned on them.

"We may not yet have seen the worst," Jan said ominously.

"And yet your masters," said Victoria, still unwilling to relinquish the floor, "provide us no additional support."

"We must find support more close by," Jan said. "We must find it where we are able. I have made other inquiries toward that end...but I feel it would be imprudent to go into more detail in such a public forum." The way he spoke the words and looked around the assembly was not an accusation that spies lurked in their midst, but rather an appeal to Camarilla loyalty.

Certainly no one would demand details of plans that might then find their way to the enemy. Victoria's facade of calm was beginning to crack as Jan took her agenda and twisted it to his own ends. Her face, usually full of healthy (and mortal-like) color, was more brightly flushed than earlier. Jan could see the wheels turning, as she reassessed her position in light of the shifting sentiment of the masses. Before she formulated a response, however, Prince Garlotte again stepped forward.

"Yes, there are many preparations still to be made," he said, "and so that we may attend to them promptly, I suggest we adjourn this conference. I would remind all guests in the city that hunting in the Inner Harbor area is strictly controlled—and that goes doubly for feeding on employees of this establishment. I direct your needs to certain neighborhoods, of which you have been made aware—Cherry Hill, McElderry Park, Broadway East..."

The assembly began to break up as small knots of Kindred formed to discuss what they'd just heard, or to complain about their lodgings, the hunting restrictions, or any other number of difficulties faced by a refugee in the city of Baltimore, which was now grossly overpopulated with undead. Jan watched them wander away discussing their situations, but one conversation more than the others attracted his attention. He had been watching the larger audience, not Victoria, when the prince had stepped in, but she seemed to have quickly recovered from her general disgruntlement as she glided through the confusion toward Aisling Sturbridge. The Tremere regent and Victoria exchanged civil greetings—Victoria with a relaxed, pleasant expression on her face; Sturbridge, for all intents and purposes, expressionless—then both turned away just enough that Jan couldn't make out what they were saying. Though the childe of Hardestadt had no fondness for English, that was not to say that he wasn't thoroughly versed in the language to the point that he could read lips—an ability that, along with reading text upside down across a desk, had proven invaluable on numerous occasions. Kindred, so caught up in their supernatural world of the undead, often overlooked such simple ploys that were within the capabilities of many mortals.

There was little point in speculating as to exactly what passed between Victoria and Sturbridge, but Jan was nevertheless curious. At the very least, the conversation, as well as the possibility of a new alliance among the ever-shifting politics of the Kindred, was worth noting.

"Mr. Pieterzoon..."

Jan turned from the ongoing conversation across the way. Robert Gainesmil stood at his side.

"The prince would speak with you," said Gainesmil, "if you can spare a few minutes, of course."

Jan shook hands with Gainesmil, the Toreador who apparently harbored ties, if not loyalty, to both the prince and Victoria. "Please, call me Jan." With his other hand, he clasped Gainesmil by the shoulder, as he might an old acquaintance. "My time, as well as my services, are always at the disposal of the prince."

The prince, indeed, had exited the chamber, and Gainesmil indicated the nearby door. "After you, Jan."

Jan inconspicuously glanced once more at Victoria and Sturbridge. The Toreador laughed at something that was said, then the two parted. Jan, ahead of Gainesmil, made his exit as well. *This will be a long night*, he thought. It was not the first, nor, he knew, would it be the last.

Saturday, 17 July 1999, 1:40 AM
Cherry Hill
Baltimore, Maryland

Fin always felt like he stuck out in this neighborhood. Probably because he did. Among the boarded-up stores and abandoned houses, he looked like a drug dealer. Riches among squalor. His new leather jacket was just too shiny, his black hair too perfect. He hated to park his Camaro on the street. Not that he wouldn't be able to track down and settle with anybody who was stupid enough to mess with his car, because he would, but then he'd have the hassle of fixing whatever damage they'd done.

I don't know why I come here anyway, he thought. Some nights he just felt restless, and the next thing he knew, he was walking up the crumbling sidewalk to the shack that looked like it was held together by nothing more than its last coat of paint—and that was chipping and peeling away in a hurry. Nights like these, it didn't do him any good to go see Morena. He loved her, but there were some things that a mortal just couldn't understand. Not that he was likely to get much sympathy here.

Jazz opened the door. "Well, if it ain't our own Boy Hollywood. Is that a new jacket? I hope you Scotch-garded it. You know how messy it gets in here." She called back into the house, "Yo, Katrina! Your fancy brother's here!"

She stepped aside and Fin went in. "I'm not her brother."

"I forget how these things work," said Jazz. "I ain't as high and mighty as some folks." She showed him a wide, hissing grin, revealing the fangs that marked her for what she was.

Tarika lounged on an old, lopsided couch that was literally

on its last leg. Her skin matched almost exactly the dark
Naugahyde. "Looking spiffy, Fin. Mind if I take your wheels for
a spin?" She and Jazz each wore loose tanktops and tight jeans.
Fin tried to ignore the two women, tried not to let on how
uncomfortable they made him. They were brash and streetsmart
and from a part of the mortal world—the bottom end of the
spectrum—that he'd never been familiar with. He didn't really
want to be familiar with it now either, but this was where
Katrina was. She sauntered into the room barefoot, wearing
only a too-tight, white T-shirt and painted-on jeans.

"What d'you want?"

Fin hesitated. He didn't know why he'd hoped for something
different. This was how it always went. The way Katrina saw it,
he had to be there for a reason. There seemed to be no chance he
could ever just hang out.

"How are you doing?" he asked.

"Same as I'm always doing." Katrina just stood there,
waiting for him to say whatever it was he'd come to say.

"How's that little pincushion of yours in the suburbs?" Jazz
whispered in his ear. "Why don't you ever bring her by?"

"She better for biting or licking?" Tarika asked with an evil
grin that showed her fangs to best effect. She rubbed the tip of
her tongue slowly over her teeth.

Fin refused to be baited. "What do you think about all the...
stuff going on? In the city, I mean. And Washington."

The question was meant for Katrina, but Tarika didn't
hesitate to answer. "Shit. They have a sale on fangs at K-Mart or
something? Can't throw a brick in this neighborhood without
hitting a damn vampire."

"Day-time folks gonna get nervous if people keep
disappearing," Jazz chimed in. "Now us, we don't kill people.
We always let 'em live and let 'em go. Need as many fish in the
pond as we can get. Ain't that right?"

"Mm-hm," Tarika agreed.

They were irritating, but in a way, Fin was almost glad that
Jazz and Tarika were there. At least they talked to him. Katrina
just stood and glared. "What do you think about it?" he asked
her.

"I don't think nothing," she said, and leveled her glare at the other two women, so they'd know they were talking more than she approved. "Those losers will move on soon enough, or maybe I'll start offing them myself, if they get in our way."

"Yeah. We got dibs on this neighborhood," Jazz said.

"I've been thinking," Fin said, "about...about maybe trying to, you know, take a more active role. I mean, our sire *is* the prince, and if there's stuff that needs to change..."

"Why you telling me this?" Katrina asked. "You do whatever you want."

"I thought I might be able to help," Fin tried to explain. "I mean, if there are too many Kindred around here, it could endanger the Mas—"

"*Kindred.*" Katrina spat the word mockingly. "What the hell is that supposed to mean anyway? Garlotte isn't my daddy, and you aren't my brother. You do whatever you want, tell them whatever you want. I don't care. We don't care."

"That's right," Jazz said, as she stepped by Fin and to Katrina's side. "We don't need none of them."

Katrina took hold of Jazz, ran a finger along her bare throat. Jazz raised her chin. "We don't need none of you," Katrina said. She ran her tongue along Jazz's neck, up over her chin. They ended with a long, lingering kiss.

Fin turned and walked out of the house. They'd made themselves clear enough. He'd been stupid to think that Katrina might ever accept him. That was what he seemed to come away thinking every time he came. Maybe a trip to Morena's would make him feel better after all.

Saturday, 17 July 1999, 1:48 AM
Lord Baltimore Inn
Baltimore, Maryland

"You take quite a few liberties in arranging for the defense of my city," said Prince Garlotte. This directly on the heels of a few perfunctory questions as to the suitability of Jan's lodgings.

The prince's straight-backed, wooden chair was elevated slightly above Jan's, giving the vague impression of a king on his throne. The two were alone. Gainesmil, much to his chagrin, had been dismissed after escorting Jan to the modest sitting room. Jan gathered his thoughts as he regarded Garlotte carefully. The prince's words did not actually convey anger, but the statement was most definitely a challenge.

"My hope," Jan said, "is that we will be able to defend all of the territory remaining to the Camarilla. Baltimore is, at present, in the foremost danger. I have endeavored to make use of contacts external to the city, as I imagined your efforts to be directed at keeping order within the city. Maintaining the Masquerade in the face of such an influx of Kindred can be no simple affair. If I have overstepped, my prince, I ask only your forgiveness and the opportunity to set matters aright."

Jan spoke casually yet respectfully. The ease of his manner belied the great importance of what came next. Though preferable, it was not necessary that he secure the complete and total cooperation of the prince. If, however, Garlotte stood squarely against Jan, there would be little room for maneuver. The situation would quickly become very complicated. And perhaps bloody. Jan would be compelled to seek support in other quarters—Victoria, Gainesmil, Sturbridge?—possibly in an attempt to oust the prince, so that Jan could carry his plans forward. And even then, there would still be the necessity of dealing with Garlotte's successor, whoever that turned out to be. So Jan watched Garlotte closely, indeed, as the prince mulled over these comments.

"You contacted the princes of New York, of Buffalo, and of Hartford," Garlotte said at last. "With whom else did you communicate?"

Jan hesitated not at all in answering. There were risks in being candid with the prince, but potentially much more danger in mincing words. "I spoke with Xaviar, justicar of Clan Gangrel," Jan said. He paused to gauge Garlotte's response. If the prince wished to allow matters of decorum to hinder their dealings, then this breach could become a major point of contention.

Jan volunteered information that might answer the prince's next question. "I spoke with him here, in the city, last night. In the interests of speed and secrecy, the justicar chose not to announce his presence."

Garlotte stiffened slightly at this. His nostrils flared, almost imperceptibly. "Does the justicar doubt my capacity for discretion?"

Jan cast his gaze downward somewhat. "I would never presume to speak for the justicar, my prince." He waited in silence.

"Nor would I presume," Garlotte said curtly, "to question the justicar's...ethics. Tell me, Ambassador Pieterzoon, does Xaviar gather an army of Gangrel to come rescue my city?"

"No, my prince." Jan met Garlotte's eyes again. "Xaviar gathers an army, but they go to defend Buffalo."

"Buffalo." The prince seemed genuinely surprised at this news, and less than pleased. His willingness to overlook Xaviar's slight to him—a small enough sacrifice if it gained a number of Gangrel to defend his city—began to fade. "And pray tell why?"

"My prince," Jan explained, "that city seems the most vulnerable—the most closely surrounded by Sabbat territory, and the most weakly defended. My concern is that if we do not garrison several cities in at least moderate strength, the enemy will prey on those scattered points—like wolves at a herd, bringing down the stragglers, the young and infirm—until we are completely isolated. Toward that end, I've spoken with the Giovanni in Boston, as well, trying to arrange mutual support for Hartford, though I've not met with complete success. The necromancers know of our predicament; they sense our weakness and feel no urgency to come to our aid, though they cannot afford to ignore our requests outright, lest we eventually prevail."

Prince Garlotte nodded slowly, his face solemn. "What you say is true."

"If I may be so bold," Jan added, sensing the prince's irritation ease, "I have contacted several of our brethren in Chicago, as well. As their city appears to be beyond the scope of these Sabbat activities, they've agreed to send a number of their underlings to help meet the threat here."

Garlotte's eyes narrowed as he stared at Jan, then a smile crept across the prince's face. "You seem to have been rather thorough, Mr. Pieterzoon. I imagine you have other advice to offer?"

Jan was careful to maintain his respectful, neutral expression and tone of voice. "If it would please the prince, I do have a few suggestions regarding related matters...."

"**M**y God!" Garlotte bellowed. "I don't know how I was able to face them! Jan Pieterzoon is too coy to show it, but he's snickering at me. All the others are too. I'm sure of it!

"Here I am—prince and master of this city, responsible for the safety of my guests. And assassins are running wild, murdering dignitaries—not on the edge of town, not in some out-of-the-way, shadowed comer of the slums, but *in my bloody haven!* How could this have happened? Tell me that. How?"

Isaac was reluctant to answer, not the least reason for which was that he didn't *have* a good answer. And then there was Dennis. Dennis kept staring at him.

Rather, Dennis's head kept staring at him.

Dennis had been Prince Garlotte's chief of security and right-hand ghoul for longer than Isaac had been Garlotte childe. Now, Dennis was just a head. An open-mouthed, wide-eyed, *staring* head, at that.

In his effort to avoid those astonished eyes, Isaac found himself reflexively stretching his fingers—closed, open; closed, open. He also found himself feeling grateful that vampiric vitae was potent enough to manage the relatively quick regeneration of certain body parts. Say, fingers.

Isaac felt fairly certain that heads were not prone to regeneration.

Prince Garlotte drummed his fingers on the arm of his wooden chair. His last question, unfortunately, had not been rhetorical.

"Assassin," Isaac said meekly.

"*What?*" Garlotte squinted, cocked his head. "Of course it was an assassin. I *know* it was an assassin. Every Kindred from here to Buffalo knows it was an assassin. Why do I bother?" He tossed his hands in the air. "Why? Why do I bother?"

Isaac felt a lump in his throat. He imagined that was a problem Dennis didn't have anymore. The sheriff licked his lips. The prince seemed completely to have missed the point Isaac was trying to make, and though the sheriff had mixed feelings about the wisdom of trying to expand upon his theory, he resented the prince's assumption of his stupidity to the point that he decided to make the attempt. "We think there was only one. One assassin-. Not assassins."

"*How in bloody hell would anyone know if there were one or one thousand? No one saw them!* No one but Victoria," Garlotte added. "And what does she do? She runs screaming out of the elevator and through the whole inn. Brilliant! Brilliant, that. My God, if she weren't the most exhilarating woman since Joan of Arc, I'd…I'd…"

Isaac felt very small. Much like a resident of Pompeii must have felt the day that Vesuvius decided to do its thing.

At *least he's yelling*, Isaac thought. When the prince *sounded* the most violent, he was generally less likely to *be* violent. Probably, after he had finished his meeting with Pieterzoon, Garlotte had calmly summoned Dennis to the sitting room and then proceeded to rip the ghoul's head off. Probably that had blunted the worst of Garlotte's fury. All the rest—the ranting, the yelling, the raving—was just winding down.

Probably.

Winding down just might take a little while. After all, the assassination itself had happened four nights ago. At the time, Garlotte had received the news calmly—always a bad sign. He'd spent every hour of each night and each day since then, no doubt, building up a head of steam.

Could be worse, Isaac decided. The prince was quite capable of building up a head of steam for years instead of nights. The mid-1980s had been that way.

Realizing suddenly that the prince had grown disturbingly quiet, Isaac hazarded a glance at his sire. To the uninitiated, Garlotte would have seemed to have regained his composure— his face was a healthier shade of pale; he was no longer trembling behind his dark beard—but Isaac knew better than to be fooled. Maybe, he decided, he could soothe the prince with hard-nosed professionalism. Isaac was, after all, the sheriff: "We suspect it was an Assamite."

"Why?" Garlotte scoffed. "Because there's a permanently dead body, and no one saw the killer? So it must be an Assamite?"

"Uh...yes."

"Hmph. You do know there happens to be a Sabbat army just down the road? Might they have an interest in murdering Tremere? I suspect so." Garlotte paused, but not for long. "All we *know* is that at least one of them had two hands. Aside from some of the Sabbat war ghouls, that doesn't narrow the bloody field very much."

Isaac was guardedly hopeful that his sire's temper might be starting to subside. Maybe keeping him talking was the right strategy. Isaac decided to try something non-controversial, something fairly innocuous: "You don't even *like* the Tremere."

The trembling started slowly. The telltale color returned to Garlotte's face. Isaac instinctively put his hands behind his back.

"My God!" Garlotte exploded. "I *don't* like the Tremere. I despise them! *But that doesn't mean I want one decapitated in my elevator!*"

Then the prince uttered the words Isaac had been waiting— hoping, *praying*—to hear: "Get out! Get out of my sight! Before I—"

"Yes, my prince."

And Isaac, ever the dutiful and obedient childe, hastened to obey.

Sunday, 18 July 1999, 12:22 AM
Seventh floor, Lord Baltimore Inn
Baltimore, Maryland

Victoria strode purposefully down the hallway. As far as she knew, she and Jan were the only Kindred whom Garlotte had afforded lodgings in the Lord Baltimore Inn itself. The prince normally frequented the establishment, but with the large number of guests in town had taken to staying on his little boat docked elsewhere. Vitel, too, had sought less central lodgings, though aside from the evenings of the conferences, the premises were rather dull. Theo Bell was constantly off doing whatever it was that kept Brujah amused, while Aisling Sturbridge had demonstrated little desire to stay in Baltimore any longer than absolutely necessary. The Tremere had pled urgent business at her chantry and returned to New York, but Victoria suspected the witch was motivated at least partially from fear, after what had happened to Sturbridge's predecessor at the conference.

Such a shame, Victoria thought, *if a little thing like an assassination makes the Tremere less enthusiastic about taking part in Camarilla affairs.* She marched on around the two quick turns near the middle of the building and on along the corridor.

Otherwise, there were no Kindred of sufficient standing to warrant a suite at the Lord Baltimore Inn. Just her at one end in the Governor's Suite, and Jan at the other in what more often served as Prince Garlotte's personal suite.

Victoria was pleased that her movements came with less stiffness and pain now. She had just come from a singularly satisfying hunt. As one of the prince's more privileged guests, she was not banned from hunting in the Inner Harbor area, and with the several touristy pubs, as well as the convention center not far away, prey was easy to come by. Tonight, with just a brief visit to an upscale bar, she'd attracted the company of three middle-aged business types. With very little encouragement, they had alternated, two keeping watch in a back alley while Victoria "pleasured" the third. She had sent them on their way with closed wounds and vague memories of some drunken encounter with a mysterious woman.

The blood, tonight and over the past few weeks, had done Victoria good. She felt physically repaired and, more importantly, nearly all the blemishes from her time among the Tzimisce were healed. The two that remained, she supposed, would simply require a bit more blood. Soon there would be no more reminders of the outrages committed upon her. As she approached Jan's door, her hand absently rose to the locket hanging from her neck.

Jan had expected to see Victoria at some point in the not-too-distant future and, as he opened the door, he was filled with a mix of dread and anticipation. Framed in the doorway, she appeared to him a life-size portrait. The long sleeves of the scarlet, off-the-shoulder gown accentuated the lustrous skin above, while the hue of the material brought out the auburn highlights of her hair. She wore no gloves tonight, and carried a small, beaded purse. The locket hanging from her neck caught the light, as did her emerald eyes.

"This would be where you invite me in," Victoria suggested playfully.

"Forgive me," said Jan. "You are the picture of loveliness."

Victoria lowered her eyes demurely as she stepped past him. He followed her into the spacious living area. Even among the precious works of art that Garlotte had collected—classical busts, paintings by Caillebotte, Cezanne, Renoir—Victoria stood out as an astoundingly perfect object of beauty.

"The prince does have stunning taste," she said. "But I suspect your choice of decor would differ slightly?"

Jan paused at this unexpected question. "I hadn't really given any thought to the matter."

"Oh, but surely your propensities don't match the prince's exactly," Victoria said, as she made her way from painting to painting. Jan hesitated. "Come now," she pressed him. "There's no insult to the prince in sharing your own...preferences."

The issue was moot to Jan. He was not about to redecorate the prince's chambers. Yet Jan felt the desire to humor Victoria, to play along in this small thing. "I'd have more...books, I suppose."

"Books, ah. Now we find out something fascinating about Mr. Jan Pieterzoon," she said. "What sort of books?"

"Corporate ledgers, or the like, I'm afraid." He waved away her question, suddenly embarrassed by his own stodginess. "Perhaps a few histories."

"No classics?" Victoria asked. She pouted out her lip a bit. "No romances?"

For several moments, Jan was able only to stare at her and blink. Finally, he managed to turn away.

"I'm afraid my assistants have retired for the evening, and I have nothing on hand to offer you...."

"I require nothing more than wit, charm, and scintillating conversation," Victoria said.

"Then I'm afraid you may have called upon the wrong person."

"You're too modest, Mr. Corporate Ledger Pieterzoon." She moved closer to him, came to within a few feet.

"Please, 'Jan' is fine."

"Well then, Jan, you would prefer that I get on to the business that brings me here?"

Jan casually turned and moved away from her. He couldn't quite think clearly when she was that close. He exaggerated his gestures as he spoke, lending another reason for him to seek unencumbered space. "I'm afraid that with all that is going on, and all that is on my mind, I am not fit company these nights, Ms. Ash."

"Come now," she said from right behind him. She'd kept pace, step for step. "If you are 'Jan', then I must insist on being 'Victoria'."

"Very well...Victoria." He sat in a chair, intentionally

avoiding the love seat that would allow her room next to him. "What may I do for you this evening?"

"I do so wish we'd had a chance to talk before the conference last night," Victoria said somewhat over-earnestly. "I'm afraid that we may have had an unfortunate misunderstanding. After all, both of us want nothing more than to turn back the ravagers of the Sabbat." When she said the word *Sabbat*, an intensity otherwise absent crept into her voice. It was the sound of cold and deep-seated hatred, but it passed as suddenly as it had arisen. "How unseemly for allies to spat among themselves."

"I want nothing more than to turn back the Sabbat," Jan agreed with part of her statement.

"And wouldn't it be so much more profitable," she asked, leaning forward and brushing his knee with her fingertips, "for us to work in concert, side by side?"

Despite himself, Jan suddenly pictured the two of them *lying* side by side, his limbs entwined with hers, and draped all around them the wreckage of bedclothes fervently cast aside. Then he found himself gazing into her eyes, and they truly were windows to her soul, beckoning him within, to share her deepest secrets, to share *with* her his innermost desires. He looked away. The room shifted dangerously. Jan felt the urge to take her hand in his, but resisted. He felt overwhelmed by a giddiness similar to that which had assailed him when he'd imbibed Hardestadt's mixture of ancient vitae. Jan drew strength from the thought of his sire, who would not tolerate failure.

I have only one need, he reminded himself. *Only one physical desire. Blood.*

"I would prefer that we work together," Jan said at last. He wasn't sure how many seconds had passed since she asked the question, but Victoria did not take issue with his deliberate response.

"Then let us take control of this war," she urged him. "No prince will be able to look beyond the needs of his own city. *We* must make the decisions."

Jan found himself thinking that she sounded very reasonable, that he might be able to help her toward this goal, but he steeled himself against persuasion.

Think, man. Think! he commanded himself. *She would create a council through which to rule, yet what could she offer the effort against the Sabbat? Would she hike up her skirt and hope to convince them to turn away from the gates of the city?* He opened his mouth to hurl that very accusation at her, to accuse her of gross opportunism. But he looked into the deep green of her eyes, and his thoughts were forced along another route.

"The princes will see that cooperation is required, that the self-interest of each one is also the self-interest of the others. That is what will save us."

Victoria sat back and crossed her arms. "You risk much on the reasonableness of princes. I have less faith in them than apparently you do. We must make sure they make the right choices."

"This is no conclave," Jan countered. "It is merely a gathering of Kindred, an unofficial conference.

We could call a damned conclave!" she insisted with sudden intensity. "It is *custom* for a justicar to call the conclave, but there are other ways. This is a time of crisis. If you and I, Sturbridge and maybe Bell called a conclave, with the number of Kindred in the city, Prince Garlotte would have little choice but to acknowledge the legitimacy of the endeavor."

"And the war," Jan extrapolated, "would be prosecuted according to votes of the conclave."

"Exactly."

"With each Kindred present enjoying an equal vote, from the lowliest Brujah neonate to Prince Garlotte himself."

"Yes."

Jan rose from his seat and began pacing around the room. "I don't understand why it is that you Americans maintain such a passion for democracy," he said with no little exasperation. "It is not a fascination that the elders in Europe share to any degree. I assure you that."

"The Kindred gathered in this city will not be bullied," Victoria said. "They won't stand for it."

At this, Jan stopped pacing and turned to face her. "Oh, won't they? Will they defy the prince who granted them sanctuary? Who even now keeps the wolves at bay?"

Though she overstated her case—after all, the majority of Cainites, like the majority of mortals, were sheep to be led—Victoria had touched on a very real concern of the prince's. With the flood of refugees, the city was overpopulated to the degree that popular unrest could prove dangerous. The rank and file Kindred, displaced from the princes and static power structures that normally maintained order, were a volatile mix. They were like a loaded gun, a poised stake, aimed directly at the prince's heart. Jan and Garlotte had spent quite some time discussing that very matter last night, and had arrived at several decisions. None of which Jan felt inclined to reveal to Victoria, especially since she was obviously courting the favor of the masses.

"Won't stand for it," Jan repeated dismissively. "Hmph. They'll stand for whatever the prince tells them to stand for. Unless, perhaps, they have an alternative." He stared pointedly at Victoria. "Are you planning to replace Prince Garlotte?"

She rolled her eyes. "Oh, don't be stupid, Jan."

He shrugged and resumed his pacing. "Somehow, I suspect your passion for democracy goes only so far as objecting to a dictatorship in which you are not dictator." Victoria looked away from him and did not respond. "Regardless, no Kindred that I know was ever Embraced by a democrat. If freedom is what you want, perhaps you should travel down the road to Washington. I hear personal freedom is all the rage with the Sabbat."

As he concluded his diatribe, Jan was feeling rather pleased with himself for having resisted Victoria's charms so completely, after getting over the first jolt of seeing her. When he looked back at her now, however, he saw something in her captivating eyes that he had not seen there before—total sincerity.

"I escaped those fiends once," Victoria intoned with such vehemence that Jan winced. "If I see them again, it will be to stand over their broken bodies."

Though she had not told him, Jan recognized the brutalized victim's thirst for revenge. The tone of her voice confirmed what he had heard from another source, but even had that source not existed, Jan would have guessed. Such was the venom contained in her words.

"I know you were captured," he said.

This appeared to surprise her, but she didn't deny his claim. Instead, she seemed suddenly weary; a great sadness came over her, pulled her shoulders downward like a great weight. "I cannot begin to tell you what…" She looked away from him. "I will not speak of it."

Her pain, still tinged with defiance, called to Jan, drew him in. He moved to her side and sat beside her on the couch. She clutched her locket as if that could undo what had happened.

"I'm much recovered, but…" Her words were choked off. A shudder wracked her body. Jan placed a comforting hand on her shoulder. Victoria turned so that her back was to him. Slowly, she reached for the zipper between her shoulder blades.

Jan's mouth and throat were suddenly so dry he didn't think he could speak if he tried. He watched as his own fingers grasped the zipper, slid it downward along its track. He moved slowly, unsure exactly of what Victoria wanted, but she didn't stop him, so he continued, below the small of her back, down to the bottom of the track at the level of her hips. She took his hand and placed it there on her body, at the lowest curve of her spine. Jan felt the silky smoothness of her skin, but he was not prepared for the tiny spur of bone that protruded from her flesh. It was no larger than a fingertip, but the skin surrounding it was red and irritated. *How?* he wondered.

I escaped those fiends once, she had said.

Fiends. Tzimisce. Sculptors of flesh. And bone.

Jan tried to pull his hand away, but Victoria held him to her. She was still slouched forward, and her gown now slid from her shoulders to lie bunched around her waist. Jan gazed upon the gently curving span of her back. From nape to hips, only the one small imperfection marred her beauty, a knob of bone drawn forth by some demonic torturer.

What else did they do? Jan wondered, but he knew he couldn't ask her, and there were no other visible signs of the torments she must have undergone. With the fingers of his other hand, he touched her just above the shoulders and traced the path of her spine. Sitting there before him, she seemed less fierce in her nakedness. *She's no threat to me*, he thought, as his hands slid to her hips, just beneath the folds of her dress. The visceral thrill he felt at touching her was a long-forgotten memory. How many decades had passed since he'd held a woman close, other than to feed? His problems seemed very distant—the Sabbat, Hardestadt, strong-willed princes, witches of the Tremere.

Toreador seductress? Part of Jan's mind rejected the epithet. How terrible her ordeal must have been. Victoria was in pain and needed comfort. She needed *him.* Yet Jan's mind was racing in many directions, and on many levels. Her emotional vulnerability allowed him to be close, but was not what attracted him. In his mind's eye, his fingers edged upward across the gentle ripples of her ribs. Then she took his hands and placed them on her breasts. Jan pulled her close, held her firmly against his chest, as Victoria leaned her head back against his cheek and moaned at his caresses.

Reality again interposed itself. Jan was, indeed, slowly sliding his hands up her sides. Victoria turned her face partially toward him and sighed. Something about the tilt of her head caught his attention. His hands stopped as he saw the tiny mark just above the line of her jaw. It was a blemish on her who had no natural blemish. Jan raised a finger to the mark, touched it lightly, and saw that the spot was in the shape of a serpent swallowing its own tail.

"What is—?"

"No!"

Victoria was away from him in an instant and several steps across the room. She clutched her gown to her chest, at the same time frantically trying to get something from her purse. Jan watched in total befuddlement as she opened a compact and dabbed powder over the spot—the serpent devouring itself—that he had touched. Before he regained complete control of his senses, Victoria had attended to her makeup, and her dress was zipped and in good order. She pulled the locket from beneath the fabric and let it again rest free against her chest.

Jan stared at her. The mark on her jaw was no longer visible. He began to doubt his own eyes. Had he actually seen it, or was the snake merely a figment of his confusion? Victoria spent several moments smoothing her dress, adjusting strands of hair.

She was as flustered as Jan was stunned.

"I'm afraid I must be going," she said and marched toward the door.

Jan did not recover in time to show her out. The door slammed, and she was gone. He stood unmoving and stared after her.

After several minutes, when he finally turned back to the room, a large figure stood against the wall on the other side of the love seat. The creature, where not covered by its threadbare suit, was hairy—short, brown fur with mangy splotches of gray. The suit might have been elegant once, many years and many more launderings ago, but seemed now barely to hold together. The creature's eyes were large and completely black—there appeared to be no white, no iris—and set far apart above the gaping hole where a nose should have been. Jagged teeth stuck through one side of its lip, so only the other side of the mouth seemed capable of opening.

"Well," it said, "that sure was a sight for sore eyes."

Jan steadied himself against the back of the chair. He felt shaky and completely unready to handle the demands placed on him. "What were we talking about before... that?"

"About *her*," said Marston Colchester. "You know, speak of the devil." He let out a wheeze that Jan had come to recognize as what would be laughter from someone with a nose. "I tell you, I been hanging out with the wrong people. Never had Victoria Ash walk into my suite and drop her panties, thank you ma'am."

Jan sat in the chair. "I believe she kept on her 'panties' for the entire visit."

"If she did, that was about the only thing. My, my. You have to admire a woman who don't wear a bra."

Jan ignored the Nosferatu's comments. Otherwise, the conversation would never progress beyond the relative merits of various feminine undergarments. This obscene creature was the first Kindred Jan had sought out upon reaching Baltimore. How, he wondered, could Prince Garlotte have ruled for so long while completely neglecting this clan? The prince professed disdain for the Nosferatu. It was a mistake many

Kindred made, including, regrettably, many Ventrue. Jan was slightly incredulous that Colchester had attended the more recent conference. Jan had looked over the auditorium rather thoroughly. How could a man of that size go unnoticed? The same way he'd just hidden himself, Jan imagined, during Victoria's visit.

Victoria. Jan needed to put her out of his mind; he needed to change the subject, or at least shift the conversation down more productive avenues. "You said you heard the conversation between Victoria and Sturbridge as the conference was breaking up?" Jan prodded.

"That I did. Now, that Tremere, she's not one to go running about with no panties on."

"The conversation—?"

"Right." Colchester settled onto the love seat and ran his fingers across the fine upholstery. "So, your girlfriend the Toreador waltzes up to Sturbridge, real sly-like and smiling the whole time, but she says something about, 'Are you Tremere going to do Ventrue bidding, and them not bothering to send any help?' And Sturbridge, she says, 'If we gotta make do with whats we already got, then we gotta make do.'"

Jan absorbed this report. The wording was obviously filtered through Colchester's own vernacular, but the meaning seemed reasonable enough.

"Then," the Nosferatu continued, "Victoria asks if Sturbridge wants to talk more about it, and Sturbridge says that she ain't sticking around. She's gotta get back to New York real quick-like."

"I see." Over the years, Jan had learned better than to question the veracity of information gathered by the Nosferatu. *Victoria has no agreement with the Tremere,* he thought. This was significant news for several reasons. The Tremere, secretive and uniformly distrusted among the Kindred, were always a potential danger. The fact that they apparently were not cooperating with Victoria made Victoria less of a threat. Also, the fact that Sturbridge herself did not seem to have much of a rapport with Victoria cut down on the likelihood that Victoria had in some way engineered or been complicit in the assassination of Maria Chin, in order that a more cooperative Sturbridge could join the conference.

Of course, there was the possibility, however slight, that they had suspected they were being watched and had orchestrated the entire conversation. "Did they meet again?" Jan asked.

"Nope. Sturbridge hightailed it for New York not too long after that."

"I see." Jan settled back into the armchair and began to massage the bridge of his nose. His fingers, however, still remembered the sensation of Victoria's supple skin. He was plagued by the ghost image that never was—his hands clasped firmly over her breasts, her body pressed back against his. He shook his head to clear away the mental picture.

I'll have to be more careful, he decided. There was no point in overestimating his ability to resist her. *I'll stay away from her, not meet with her in private.* But such thoughts raised a dull ache in his chest. If only there weren't the political games.... *If there weren't political games, she wouldn't be interested in you,* he reminded himself.

"Marston, can you watch her the next few nights?" Jan asked.

The Nosferatu rubbed his hairy palms together. "Since it's for a good cause." The twisted grin of his half-pierced lip sent a chill through Jan.

There was no need to show Colchester out. He was simply no longer there. Jan busied himself trying to arrange all the pieces of the puzzle in his mind, and trying *not* to think about one particularly beautiful piece of that puzzle.

Monday, 19 July 1999, 2:12 AM
Federal Hill
Baltimore, Maryland

"Would you like to stroll up the hill, sir?" Marja asked.
"No." Jan felt confined. Never mind that there was plenty of room in the limousine, even with himself and both assistants. Marja leaned away from him and toward Roel as she gazed out the passenger's side window at the park beyond.

"It's a nice night, sir," added the driver, Herman. His partner, Ton Baumgarte, in the front passenger seat, nodded agreement.

"Mr. Abbeel," Jan said evenly to the driver, "should I require advice of a recreational nature from you, rest assured that you will be among the first to know."

Herman returned his attention to Key Highway. The limousine moved slowly along. There was little enough traffic and, even if Jan wasn't, Marja and Roel seemed to be enjoying this night-time tour of the city. The car itself was a regular rental. Among all the other arrangements and contacts, Jan had seen no immediate need to have his own armored and light-sealed vehicle shipped from Amsterdam and, in fact, tonight had been the first occasion since arriving that he'd desired the use of an automobile. He'd required precious little of his two assistants over the last three nights. The contacts and negotiations had all been with Kindred, requiring Jan personally—no "legitimate" business interests—and so the mortals' presence had been rendered moot in that regard.

There remained, of course, the need to feed. Jan glanced at Marja. As she leaned over Roel to look out the window, the taut muscles of her neck drew the vampire's notice—sternomastoid, sternohyoid, omohyoid—and tucked among them the pulsating jugular. Jan had been so busy the past few nights that he'd neglected to feed, and how he could feel the hunger rising.

Perhaps that's why I was so...susceptible to Victoria last night, he started to consider, but then pushed that entire topic from his thoughts.

This drive was not, after all, a field trip to amuse his servants. Jan had thought he wanted company, though now he was having second thoughts. What he'd wanted most, he realized, was to be away from the Lord Baltimore Inn; more specifically, away from the seventh floor and the suite at the opposite end of the building from his own. He'd accomplished much since receiving this impossible assignment from Hardestadt. A casual drive through the city should have been a pleasant enough distraction. Yet here Jan was, feeling hemmed in by his sight-seeing retainers, and thinking about the one person he wanted not to think about.

Damned Toreador.

Jan couldn't help remembering the tiny mark on Victoria's jaw, the serpent devouring its own tail. It was pure chance that he'd seen it. And Victoria's reaction—that was the strangest of all. New concerns began to take shape in Jan's mind. A *Tzimisce symbol... Could it be that she...?* But Jan had difficulty focusing his thoughts. He also couldn't help remembering the perfect curves of Victoria's naked back, the luster of her skin, the delicate ripple of her ribs beneath his fingers....

"What is this place?" Jan asked Marja. Anything was better than thinking, than remembering. He gestured toward the grassy rise that she'd suggested climbing.

"Federal Hill," she said.

"During the American Civil War it was a fort, of sorts," explained Roel. The young man was as able an executive assistant as was Marja, and another source of nourishment to boot. Neither was aware of the other's similar, unofficial capacity, or of the common link that made them so valuable to Jan.

I will feed as soon as we get back, Jan thought. It was not wise to neglect his own welfare, and it seemed he might need his strength in the upcoming weeks if Victoria continued to challenge both his authority and his control over himself.

Herman did not see in time the large figure that stepped out into the street just in front of the car. The impact jolted all the passengers. Jan instantly forgot all thoughts of Federal Hill, of Victoria. The dual airbags inflated and shoved Herman and Ton back against their seats. No one in the back was wearing a seatbelt. Jan and his assistants slammed into the seats before them.

"Oh my God," Marja said, picking herself up from the floor. "We hit someone." Then she noticed the blood gushing from Roel's nose. Jan noticed as well. "Roel, you're bleeding. Are you—?"

Her question was cut off by the bullets that started tearing through the car. The passenger's-side windows shattered. A spray of automatic gunfire ripped apart Ton and Roel. Glass, blood, and bullets were everywhere at once. Marja jerked spasmodically as she was hit. She was knocked back onto Jan, and he against the door. Bullets exploded through his arms, his chest, his face.

Herman freed himself from the deflating airbag and flung his door open. Jan reached for his door handle a split second after his driver managed to stand and raise his own semi-automatic pistol, aiming across the roof of the car at their assailant. But Herman was slammed into the car from behind. His weapon clattered to the ground, and he slumped after it with a small arrow completely through his neck.

Not an arrow, Jan realized. A stake.

Jan's door was open, but instead of fleeing, he used it as a shield. He grabbed Herman's gun and flung himself back through the car, over the bodies of Marja and Roel—away from whomever had fired the stake. The gunman on the other side of the car was surprised to see Jan coming straight at him through the shattered window, and even more surprised as Jan unloaded the pistol's clip into him. Jan had never practiced with one of these modern weapons. He was as surprised as the gunman, whose chest and neck seemed to explode.

Jan forced himself the rest of the way through the window

as his assailant collapsed in a heap. The Ventrue's first instinct was to flee, but then he saw the assault rifle in the hand of the inert gunman. Jan dropped the empty pistol and grabbed the new weapon. He whirled toward the front of the limousine. The creature that the car had hit stood unharmed among the wreckage of the bumper and grille.

War ghoul, Jan thought, though he couldn't be sure. He'd never seen one up close before, but it was too damned big to be completely human; that and it had a large horn sticking up from the middle of its forehead. The effect was more rhinoceros than unicorn.

Jan let loose with the rifle. Dozens of bullets chewed into the hood of the car, the pavement. A tire exploded. So did a streetlight half a block away. Jan blew to hell everything in sight—everything except the ghoul. And then the gun stopped firing.

"Shit."

Jammed? Out of ammo? Didn't much matter. Jan ran for the grassy knoll. After the first few yards, he remembered that somebody back there was firing stakes—out of a shotgun? A crossbow? So Jan tried to weave as he ran, not to make too steady a target. It might have been a good idea, but he almost managed to trip himself, and quickly gave it up.

At the top of the hill, he paused and looked back. Three shapes were pursuing him up the slope of the park: the rhinoceros, another more human-sized figure, and a creature on all fours. Jan tried the assault rifle again. He pointed the gun and kept pressing the trigger, but no more shots fired.

"Shit."

He threw the weapon to the ground, then turned and fled in earnest.

Sabbat.

The word bounced through his mind every few steps.

Sabbat.

But how could they have sneaked into Baltimore with all the patrols operating north of Washington?

They couldn't have. But somebody had sure as hell just shot up his staff.

Sabbat.

Shot up his staff? Shot up *him!*

As Jan wove among the trees on the crest of the small hill, he tried to take stock of his injuries. At the very least, he was still mobile. Otherwise, he'd probably have been destroyed by now. He thought for a brief moment of Marja and Roel and Ton, their blood pooling in the floorboards of the limousine, and of Herman lying on the pavement pierced by a wooden stake. But there was no time for sentimentality. Survival must come first.

The bullet wounds Jan had suffered were painful but luckily not disabling. He tried to pinpoint the holes, to direct healing vitae to the worst of them. A few bullets that had lodged near the surface popped out as shallow wounds filled. Other slugs would just have to stay in him for the time being. If he survived, he could have them cut out later. One bullet had passed through both cheeks and shattered a few teeth en route. Another had managed to tear away most of an ear. Again, painful but not fatal. Jan lost count somewhere around fifteen bullets. Nothing blood wouldn't take care of.

What blood? he wondered, fighting off a wave of desperation. The little healing he'd done had taken its toll, and though he was more whole of body, he now felt fatigue beginning to overtake him. He thought for a moment about circling back, about trying to get to Marja and Roel before they were completely cold, but the assassins might have left a guard for just that reason, and Jan couldn't hope to win a straight-up fight at this point.

Holding the fatigue at bay, Jan kept running out of the park and through the neighborhoods to the south. He cut down a side street, then turned south again, pausing at the corner of a building to watch. He didn't have long to wait before they turned the first corner. The large dog-like creature was first, sniffing along the ground. *Following my scent,* Jan realized. The next stalker held the leash attached to the dog-thing. Finally, Rhino brought up the rear. He seemed to be limping slightly. Maybe the limo had injured him—but the car had definitely gotten the worse end of the deal.

Jan watched for a moment longer, hoping they would make a wrong turn, but the bloodhound was following his path exactly.

Jan ran again. Each step took more out of him. He cursed himself for having not fed for so many nights. If he had more blood, he might be able to swing wide to the west, to make a large circle, not to the car, but back to the Lord Baltimore. Surely he could find help there. But Jan's strength was fading fast. He'd never make it so far.

And wouldn't Garlotte love for me to run through the lobby of his hotel with a Sabbat hit squad on my tail, Jan thought. Thought of imperiling the Masquerade led his mind back to the limousine and the four bodies in and around it. There was no way for Jan to hide that little faux pas. *Garlotte will just have to clean that up.*

Jan stopped again. He shook his head, trying to purge all extraneous thought—he didn't have time to worry about feeding, or Garlotte, or the Masquerade—but mostly he just succeeded in shaking loose another piece of broken tooth. Ahead of him was another park. Beyond it, more docks. He'd crossed the neck of this narrow peninsula. He couldn't see his pursuers at the moment, but he had a sick feeling that they were still back there, that they were still tracking him. The bloodhound wouldn't lose his trail, and the Sabbat wouldn't give up. The park, he decided, had nothing to offer. If he climbed into a tree or tried to hide, they would track him down. Maybe near the docks he would run across some roving band of Brujah. Beyond that, he didn't have much of a plan. Or much hope.

Lox pulled at the lead constantly, but Terrence held him back. *There's no reason for it to have come to this,* Terrence thought. *No reason for us to have to track this bozo across the city.* But Sonny had bungled his job. Terrence had been surprised when Euroboy gunned down Sonny, but not too upset. Sonny was an ass. He deserved whatever he got. Apparently Blaine had anticipated something like this happening. That's why Terrence and Lox were there.

Even holding back Lox, Terrence was outpacing Jammer. In stopping the limo, the horned monstrosity seemed to have busted a knee, and without Bolon or Vykos or—God forbid—the Little Tailor around, there was no one to fix it *.Jeez.* Terrence shuddered just thinking of those high-octane Tzimisce. He was just as glad that they weren't there. Sure they were clanmates and all, but they creeped the hell out of him.

Let Jammer limp, Terrence thought. The big idiot should've known better than to use himself as a human—relatively speaking—roadblock. *But, hey, you tell him to stop a car, he stops the car.* After all, Blaine didn't pick Jammer for his manners, savvy, or conversational skills.

Lox jerked more energetically at his lead.

"Stop your grunting, you stupid idget." Terrence gave the creature a swift kick in one of its malformed, canine legs. Lox had been a friend, a fellow Tzimisce, before an egregious foul-up had led Vykos to turn him into the slavering bloodhound-of-a-thing he was now. *Easy come, easy go,* thought Terrence. Compared to some who pissed off Vykos, Lox had gotten off light.

Lox's agitation meant that the trail was getting fresher. Euroboy was slowing down. *Running out of steam,* Terrence thought. Maybe Sonny had pegged him a few times before he bought the farm. Of course, Sonny probably wasn't mangled beyond repair—if Blaine thought that some screw-up Lasombra was worth the trouble. Terrence wouldn't bet on Sonny's chances.

He wouldn't bet on Euroboy's chances either. Jammer was almost caught up now. "Come on, you stupid, horny bastard," Terrence called, and then let Lox lead the way again. The bloodhound tugged at the leather straps. He sniffed back and forth along the trail so energetically that he set his testicles swinging side to side.

Their prey's course veered left of the upcoming park, to Terrence's surprise. *Figured we'd find him curled up under a bush calling for daddy.* Ahead were some of the city's docks, but that wasn't going to save Euroboy. He couldn't hide behind the smell of water and diesel, or the sound of cranes and forklifts. Not for long. Lox would sniff him out.

Terrence didn't bother with trying to conceal himself. He looked fairly normal, and Lox could be mistaken for some kind of big fucking dog. And if anybody wanted to stop Jammer and ask him why he was so ugly, they were welcome to it. Mostly, Terrence didn't care who saw him. This was a Camarilla city. If he stirred up a little trouble for the limp-wristed Ventrue prince to cover up, that was just hunky-damn-dory. *Dock workers don't care anyway*, Terrence figured. *They're just doing their grunt job and collecting union wages.*

The trail led right down to the access road along the water's edge. With Jammer not too far behind, they began to pass piers. Ships were docked at most, and many were loading or unloading cargo. *24-7*, Terrence thought. *Fucking grunts. At least I get days off.*

Lox was about to lose it. He strained to get away from his keeper and snarled insanely. "Pipe down, you moron. You're gonna gag on your own spit." It had happened before.

Terrence paused alongside one of the big ships. He held Lox in check and scanned their surroundings. A large crane was unloading pallets, swinging its load slowly over the access road. Jammer was caught up to within a few yards. Lox jerked frantically at the lead, redoubling his efforts to get free.

"Oh yeah, we're close," Terrence muttered to himself. "I'm gonna pin Euroboy's ears to his—"

Lox gave an incredible tug. Terrence lost his balance and stumbled forward. He fell to his knees and was dragged by the bloodhound, just as the huge pallet from the crane crashed to the ground where they'd been standing. The force of the impact bounced Terrence into the air. He landed roughly and stared at the wreckage. He'd seen it happen. One second Jammer was limping toward him; the next second forty fucking tons of broken crates and spilled sugar were spread over the goddamned dock where Jammer had been.

Terrence had the leather lead wrapped around his wrist, so while he was staring at the mountain of sugar that had almost crushed him like it had Jammer, Lox was about to dislocate his shoulder pulling in the other direction. After a few seconds, the pain got Terrence's attention. He turned just in time to see Euroboy scurry up the gangplank and onto the sugar boat. Terrence freed his hand from the lead. "Rip his heart out," he said.

Lox was off in an instant, charging up the gangplank.

The crane operator had evened the odds slightly. Though Jan had hoped for better, he was more refined than to be ungrateful. The sight of Rhino crushed beneath the huge pallet was sweet indeed. But Jan only allowed himself a few seconds to admire his handiwork. The bloodhound and his master still survived. Jan would have been better off if the…the whatever that thing was that was following his scent had been destroyed. It wasn't a dog. Now that Jan saw it at closer quarters—as close as he wanted to get—it seemed vaguely humanoid, though bent over on all fours, legs deformed so that they were much like a canine's, and its face grotesquely flattened.

Tzimisce, Jan thought. Or some foul creation of that clan.

If the bloodhound had been destroyed, Jan might have slipped away and made his way back to allies eventually. But the Sabbat could still follow his trail, and Jan had no doubt they would.

Before the beast's handler had time to raise himself off the ground, Jan dashed up the gangplank of the closest freighter. As he crossed the deck, he heard the baying of the hound behind him, coming closer. There was more activity on board than Jan would have preferred. A small crowd, alarmed by the tremendous crash of the sugar pallet, had gathered near the railing. Jan had no idea how something like the bestial creature trailing him might be explained away. But suddenly the Masquerade became much less of a concern as the hound crested the gangplank and galloped onto the deck. Different clusters of mortal onlookers had exactly opposite reactions: some froze, paralyzed by terror; others ran for their lives. Jan ran too, and the shouts and confusion provided some cover.

The hound only paused for a moment, however, before it was after him again. It had his scent and wasn't about to be thrown off by a few frantic mortals. One sailor stumbled before the onrushing beast. It didn't slow in the slightest. Its hind claws raked deep into the sailor's body as the creature rushed on after Jan. With a few powerful bounds, it closed the distance between them. Jan could feel it gaining on him. It was practically on him, so close that the beast's snarls reverberated in his chest.

Jan lunged for the nearest doorway on the ship's superstructure just as the beast leapt for him.

He slammed the hatch. The force of the hound's impact against the door knocked Jan backward. The sound of the blow set the metal bulkheads humming. But the door held. Jan slammed home the heavy bolt and backed slowly away, all the while watching the door, as the beast pounded and clawed on the opposite side.

Jan forced himself to turn away from the blocked portal, to take note of his surroundings. He was in a corridor, not a single cabin. *Thank God for that*, he thought. He wasn't trapped. But that also meant that the hound could still get to him, and probably it would set about that as soon as it realized the door between them was impassable. *If* the door between them remained impassable and didn't tear from its hinges any second. Either way, Jan had to move.

He started down the corridor, but now that the hound was not right behind him, he began to grow lightheaded. The arrow-straight passage seemed to zig and to zag. Blood. Jan had to find some soon. The wounds he'd suffered would definitely have killed a mortal, and would have destroyed—or incapacitated, which amounted to the same thing—many a Kindred. Jan had only the blood of Hardestadt and the elders of Clan Ventrue to thank that he'd survived this long. He might shrug off two dozen gunshots for a time, but eventually he'd have to find more blood. And for him, in a foreign land, that could prove difficult, because the blessing of Clan Ventrue resilience was accompanied by a curse that burdened no other clan. If only he could just grab the first sailor he came across and drain him—inelegant, yes, but style mattered very little at times like these—but it could not be.

Move, damn you! Jan told himself.

Blood, though vital, was not his most immediate problem. He couldn't tell if the howling at the door had abated, and he wasn't going to take the time to find out. Then he saw what he was looking for—a ladder. He paused for a moment, then started climbing down. One level, two. But he found that he had to concentrate on the ladder or he missed rungs, and he soon lost track of how far he'd descended.

Finally, even though he was careful with placement of hands and feet, he misstepped.

For a moment that seemed to encompass lifetimes, he felt himself in freefall. He passed beyond the tangible world, felt himself free of it—then his hands grabbed hold. He jerked to a halt, smashed his face on the side of the ladder. He stayed there longer than he could afford to, clutching the rungs like a prodigal child might embrace his mother.

A few more steps down and Jan stumbled into another corridor. The lightheadedness gave way to debilitating vertigo. Jan staggered. He didn't even see the sailor before the young man caught him and kept him from falling to the floor. The yellow lights below deck seemed unusually harsh to Jan. He squinted up at the sailor.

"Are you all right, sir?"

But Jan barely heard the words. They were drowned out by the rhythmic rush of blood beneath the boy's skin. So much blood, so close, and of so little use to Jan. He latched onto the boy, struggled to his feet.

"Where is the engine room?" Jan asked, his voice barely a whisper.

The sailor was puzzled. "Do you need a doctor?"

"*Where is it?*" Jan hissed. He held tight as the boy recoiled from him, the mortal's mind suddenly confronted with that which it couldn't comprehend. "The engine room."

"This way," said the sailor, pointing down the corridor. "Not far." There was no fear in his voice, only obedience.

"Take me there," said Jan.

The boy was quite amenable, much like the crane operator had been. Jan never could have figured out the crane controls in time, nor in his current state could he have found the engine room on his own.

As they made their way along the corridor, Jan tried to listen for sounds of the bloodhound, but his ears were ringing. He couldn't be sure if what he heard were really the beast's snarls from the deck just above, the sound of the creature's claws as it slid down a ladder in pursuit. Or were the noises in his own head? With each step, Jan expected the hound to pounce on him from behind. Finally, he and the sailor reached the engine room.

"Is there another exit?" Jan asked.

The sailor nodded. "Three. One on the far end, this level. Two on the catwalk, either side."

"Crew?"

The boy glanced at his watch. "No. Shouldn't be."

Jan leaned against the nearby doorway. *Good*, he thought. He had enough lives on his conscience for one night. This boy would follow his instructions without question; if Jan was lucky, they'd both survive. If he wasn't lucky...well, then at least he wouldn't have to worry about his conscience. Jan rested there against the doorway for a minute or two. He inspected the door itself and the emergency panel on the wall just inside the engine room.

Then a chilling howl echoed down the corridor—the cry of a hunter who'd caught the scent of his prey. The boy looked nervously back the way they'd just come. Jan placed a calming hand on his shoulder, though Jan felt no great sense of calm himself. He waited a few moments longer. The howl sounded again, closer. The hound was definitely tracing their path.

"Come on," Jan said at last. He half led, half supported himself on the boy as they made their way across the engine room. The main thoroughfare through the buzzing, vibrating machinery was a relatively straight shot, but the engine room was long, about fifty meters. If it was *too* long, or if it were too short, for that matter, then Jan knew that he and the boy were finished. The mortal kept glancing back over his shoulder—and then his eyes suddenly grew wide with fear.

"Come on, damn you!" Jan urged the youth to greater speed, though it was Jan's infirmity that slowed them. He caught the boy's eye, put all his waning energy into maintaining his control. If he faltered and the sailor fled, there'd be no hope.

The engine room seemed to stretch on and on before them. It seemed that each step took them nowhere. Finally, when Jan guessed they were at least halfway, he did risk a glance back. They were well over halfway, in fact, but entering the other door were the hound and his master. The master again had the leash in hand.

Don't turn it loose, Jan thought. *Just don't let go.*

Jan took the boy's chin in his hand, looked deep into his eyes and spoke words that must be obeyed if either of them were to survive: "Run. Hit the emergency fire code. Wait for me just beyond the door. *Now.*"

The boy was anxious to obey—anxious to run, at least. But his running was a prompt to the hound's keeper. He turned loose the leash.

"Kill, Lox!"

The beast didn't need instruction, might not even have heard its master. It shot across the long, narrow chamber. Jan ran as well. He'd waited only a second after the boy ran, but it seemed as if everyone else were moving at full speed while Jan labored in slow motion. He followed the sailor toward the door and prayed that his legs wouldn't fail him.

The boy reached the emergency panel, jabbed in the code, and was out the door in record time. By the time Jan got close to the exit, the emergency fire door was sliding down—a quarter of the way, halfway. He could hear the hound closing the distance between them, and the keeper was all the while yelling, "Kill, Lox! Kill!"

Jan pictured the door closing before he could get through. He pictured it not closing in time to trap the hound. He pictured the beast taking him down before he got to the door. Jan's legs were numb. They must've functioned on their own, because he couldn't feel them. Still several meters from the doorway, Jan dove and rolled. The fire door was well past half closed. It would meet the floor in a few seconds and Jan would be trapped or crushed.

The beast howled and lunged for Jan just as he slid under the door. The creature caught his leg. Its claws sank in, dug into his flesh as it pulled itself along. His leg and the beast's upper body were directly beneath the door. Half a meter farther and it would be sealed.

Jan twisted around just in time to see the sailor swinging a fire extinguisher through the air. The butt end of the metal container smashed the hound square in the face. Bones cracked. The beast grimaced and spat blood but didn't let go of Jan's leg.

Jan kicked at the monster with his free foot with little effect. The beast seemed only angered by the attacks and sank its fangs into Jan's leg. At the same time, the sailor swung the fire extinguisher again.

Jan and the beast both howled in pain. Teeth clattered across the floor. The hound pulled back its smashed face. Jan pulled his broken ankle free of the doorway just as the fire door ground completely closed.

Jan fell back on the floor. He closed his eyes against the pain jolting through his ankle and leg and allowed himself one prolonged roar of agony. As the echoes of his scream died away, he noticed the strange silence—strange because there was no pounding and scratching from the other side of the fire door.

"Are all the exits closed?" Jan asked to be sure.

The boy nodded. His mouth hung open slightly, but he was mute from what he'd seen.

Jan struggled up onto his elbows to inspect the damage to his ankle—and saw the two amputated, clawed hands that still clung to his leg. Blood had soaked into the cuff of his pants leg. The dizziness that he'd overcome during the height of the danger returned now with a vengeance. Jan lay back down.

His mind was still racing. *They might bypass the system. They might get the doors open, or find another exit, a vent system.* There was no time to be lost, but only with great effort was he able to sit up again. Gingerly, he plucked the claws from his skin, his clothing, and tossed the hands away.

"Help me up." It was necessary, but neither pleasant nor comfortable. "Take me to the captain," said Jan. "Now. And once we're there, go find me a damned crutch."

The handful of sailors helped Jan down the gangplank. They had no idea who this battered visitor limping along on his crutch was. They only knew that orders were orders, and the captain had ordered them to see this person off the ship. Their careful glances showed their unease. They wondered if his presence had anything to do with the crane accident, or with the rabid dog that had gotten on board. But they asked no questions, nor did they linger on the dock. The ship's engines were roaring to life. The men hurried back on. The ship cast off almost at once.

Jan skirted the crowd assembled around the wreckage of the sugar crates. An ambulance had pulled up—little need for that—but no police. No one seemed to know exactly what had happened. An investigation would be required, safety procedures reviewed in depth. No dock workers were unaccounted for, but a few people insisted that the load had fallen on *someone*. Eventually, Jan knew, they would dig into the huge pile, haul away the sugar and sacks and splintered wood, and the compressed mass of unidentifiable body parts would cause quite a stir.

Garlotte will have to take care of that too, Jan thought. The prince would have to see that his people explained away the accident. And the bullet-riddled limousine and five bodies. And the freighter that shoved off for sea without clearance because the captain had believed a fire in the engine room would lead to an explosion, and he was willing to sacrifice himself and his crew to ensure the safety of countless dock workers. When authorities determined that there was no fire, the captain, despite his heroic intentions, would be reprimanded, and fired. Obviously he must've been drunk or worse. But he had served his purpose.

I must get word to the prince, Jan thought. Garlotte would need to send a team in to "fumigate" the engine room, of course. Hopefully the hound and its keeper wouldn't escape before then.

All in all, not a very good night for the Masquerade. If Jan were a Kindred of less standing, he would certainly be flogged, at the very least. But as a child of influence—and, more importantly, a childe of Hardestadt—his transgressions would be overlooked. He would be lauded as a destroyer of Sabbat assassins, where a neonate, despite a lack of options, would have been punished for imprudence.

Jan staggered away from the docks and between two gray warehouses. Each step set loose tremors of pain from his ankle. He was glad to be away from the throng of mortals; he was too conspicuous limping about with bullet holes in his clothes, in his face. And the aroma of the kine was a cruel taunt. Jan thought of Marja, of Roel, of their needed blood that was denied him. There were others available—in Amsterdam. One phone call would solve the problem eventually, but that didn't help tonight.

He wandered on through South Baltimore, noticing only vaguely the street signs he passed.

Winder, Wells, Barney, Heath.

Swing west, he reminded himself. He mustn't pass too closely to Federal Hill, the limousine, the bodies. Police would be there by now.

Charles, Olive, Hanover, Clarkston.

Jan thought he'd changed directions, more or less, but he couldn't concentrate, couldn't picture in his mind the layout of the city or the relation of street to street. There was water not too far ahead, but being on a peninsula, that didn't much narrow down where he might be. The larger warehouses by the docks had given way to more modest storage buildings, one very much like the next, cinderblock or siding, blank walls, gray in the morning darkness. Or maybe Jan's mind couldn't grasp the details that distinguished one structure from another.

He heard a car in the distance, not very close, but Jan felt the sudden, illogical fear that someone would find him. He hobbled as quickly as the pain and his crutch would allow between two of the buildings, then leaned heavily against a metal wall.

Rest, he told himself. *Just for a few minutes.* Though he knew rest without blood was pointless. He let his fingers relax. The crutch slid away from him along the metal wall, clattered to the ground. Slowly, Jan slid down until he sat on the gravel.

Just a few minutes.

Jan's mind began to wander.

The Sabbat are delinquent malcontents. Have been from the beginning. Hardestadt's words were as clear as if he stood over Jan that very moment. *Return them to their place. And try not to be too long about it.*

"Return them yourself, you hoary old bastard," Jan muttered. Any minute now, he was going to get up again, to continue on his way north and around the Inner Harbor to the Lord Baltimore Inn. There was no time to waste. Hardestadt was waiting. But sitting on the ground, leaning against the building, was such a relief. Jan's ankle throbbed with only a dull ache, instead of the lightning strikes of sharp pain. And his head was swimming. He didn't know if he could go on. But he had to. Any minute now.

"You should've stayed in Europe," said Hardestadt. Jan nodded weakly in agreement. "Where the vampires are old and tired and slow."

Old and tired and slow. The words prodded Jan from his fog of pain and exhaustion. *That doesn't sound like Hardestadt.* And *vampire.* Jan's sire never used that vulgarism; always *Kindred* or *Cainite.*

Jan looked up. His immediate surroundings again asserted their reality. He was in Baltimore, near the docks, and with too little blood in his injured body. He'd just defeated, or at least eluded, a Sabbat pack. Or had he?

"Any final words, Mr. Jan Pieterzoon?"

The voice was familiar and, as Jan's eyes focused, so was the face and form. "Blaine."

"You remember. How touching." The assassin would have towered over Jan even if the smaller Ventrue weren't on the ground.

"I never forget a clanmate," Jan said.

"Clanmate, hmph. Fuck you, clanmate."

And, figuratively speaking, that's exactly what Blaine was about to do. He held a crossbow leveled at Jan's chest. A wooden bolt, like the one that had claimed Herman, would serve as a stake. Jan tried to think, but his mind was sluggish. His only chance was to dodge at just the right second and hope to take the bolt in the shoulder instead of the heart. But Blaine was so close. There would only be the smallest fraction of a second. And if Jan succeeded, then what? He lacked the strength to escape or to overpower his adversary.

"It's not too late to redeem yourself," Jan said. "You'd be valuable to the Camarilla, with your knowledge of the Sabbat."

Blaine laughed out loud. "I may be a rat, but I'm not dumb enough to jump *onto* a sinking ship."

"Your masters will want to find out what I know." Jan was

grasping at straws. He didn't relish the idea of Tzimisce torture, but short-term survival was the immediate concern. As long as he wasn't destroyed, he might still escape.

"Don't worry," said Blaine. "They know what you know. Besides, it's not like we need any help wiping—"

He never finished the sentence. Before Jan's eyes, a dark blur knocked the end of the crossbow downward. The bolt fired and sprayed gravel at Jan's feet. In the same instant, the dark figure struck Blaine in the head. The renegade Ventrue slammed into the wall behind him and collapsed to the ground.

Jan's mind took a few seconds to catch up. Standing above him instead of Blaine was a large black man in mirrored sunglasses. His heavy leather jacket seemed to swallow what little light there was. Jan knew the large man, recognized the face.

Theo Bell.

It finally sank in. Bell held a sawed-off shotgun, the reinforced stock dirtied by fresh blood. Jan glanced over at Blaine's inert body, noted the corresponding crater in his forehead.

"You gonna make it?" Bell asked.

Jan couldn't answer. He was still reconstructing how Bell had knocked the crossbow off target and then crushed Blaine's skull before either of the Ventrue had realized the Brujah warrior was there.

Jan stared at Blaine's crumpled and bloody face. The assassin, like his clanmate Jan, could no doubt withstand tremendous physical damage, yet Bell's blow had crushed the front of his head like a rotten walnut. Jan looked again at the looming Brujah.

"What about the others?" Bell asked.

"On the ship," Jan tried to explain. "Sealed in the engine room, or they were, at least. The captain's taking them out to sea." They might escape, or free themselves and take over the ship, but they were out of the way for the moment. "Another crushed on the docks. Another..." Jan started to point but was completely disoriented. His finger stabbed weakly at the air. "Was with my car. Shot. But might've recovered."

"I took care of that one," Bell said without elaboration. "Any

others that you know of?" Jan shook his head. "Okay," said Bell.
"That's all I saw too."

Then Bell stuck the barrel of his shotgun in Blaine's slack
mouth and pulled the trigger. The explosion jolted Jan back to
his senses.

"Let's go," said Bell. "Here." He retrieved Jan's crutch and
handed it to him, then stalked back toward the street and left
Jan to hobble along behind.

Jan knew that he should follow. The gunshot might very
well attract attention, and in his current condition he wouldn't
be a match for mortal police, much less for any other Sabbat
that might be lurking about. But the smell of blood was strong,
almost overpowering in the tight area. And it wasn't mortal
blood, which Jan had to be so careful about. This was vampiric
blood. Kindred vitae. Transformed by the curse of Caine into
the most tempting, and the most damning, of nectars.

Jan's hunger overcame his exhaustion and pain.

He crawled the few feet to the headless mess that had been
Blaine. Lines of blood trickled down the wall behind the body.
Such a waste, Jan thought, but he was more intent on what had
not been wasted. He took hold of a limp arm and gave in to the
hunger.

When Jan reached the street, he moved a bit more steadily.
He'd not completely drained the body but instead had torn
himself away from the rich libation as soon as he'd been able.
His ankle still pained him. The healing vitae had repaired the
injury to the point that he could more readily support his own
weight, but Jan had feared there was time for little else. The
street was completely empty, but for how long? Someone could
easily have heard the gunshot. The blast still echoed in Jan's
ears. The shotgun had been so close, it might as well have been
a cannon in the narrow space between the buildings. So Jan had
marshaled his will and made do with maddeningly few gulps.
Even now, it was all he could do to deny his inner demon, which
rebelled at the abandonment of vitae. With each step and the
increased distance it brought from the broken vessel that was
Blaine, Jan's mastery over the ravenous Beast grew stronger.

Bell was nowhere to be seen. While Jan was trying to regain

his bearings so he could begin limping back to the inn, the roar of an engine was growing dangerously close. He edged back into the shadows again, but the motorcycle screeched around the corner. Jan froze—he had not recouped enough strength to fight or even to flee—then saw that the rider, thankfully, was Bell. The Brujah came to an abrupt stop next to Jan.

"Get on."

Painfully, Jan climbed onto the motorcycle. "I have to see the prince," he started to explain. "The police—"

"Already taken care of," Bell said. He gunned the engine and they were off.

Monday, 19 July 1999, 4:36 AM
Presidential Suite, Lord Baltimore Inn
Baltimore, Maryland

Jan closed the double doors lightly, as if concerned that the soft click of the latch could somehow interrupt the muffled screams on the far side. He tried to forget that the bedroom, one of three off the main living area, existed at all. Certain unpleasantries could not be delayed, and currently he had no time for personal infirmities, physical or moral.

The carpet in Prince Garlotte's suite seemed unusually thick. Jan feared he might sink into it and be lost forever. Or perhaps it was merely his legs that threatened to give way with each step. Not since the night of his Embrace could he remember ever having felt so weak, so bone weary. He'd stumbled getting off Theo Bell's motorcycle. *I shouldn't have thrown away the crutch*, Jan had thought. He'd discarded it during the ride to the inn. His senses reeling with the heady taste of vitae lingering in his mouth, he'd misjudged the extent of his recovery. Kindred blood was powerful, but he'd taken in relatively little. He would need more blood for his wounds to heal completely, and if his ankle did not mend properly, it would require surgery at some point several months or years down the road, when time allowed. That possibility was more an inconvenience than a danger. Jan had access to some of the best doctors in western Europe. He would be whole eventually.

At the moment, however, he was having difficulty navigating among the exquisite furniture in the living room. Similarly, less than an hour ago as he'd staggered in a rear entrance of the inn, he'd had difficulty concentrating even enough to convince the mortal night manager—*assistant* night manager—to do what Jan needed him to do.

But now the deed was done. Or at least it was being done. As it had been countless times before, albeit Jan's current arrangements were rather clumsy and heavy-handed. He'd had little choice. He'd made the necessary call to Amsterdam as soon as he'd entered the suite, but he didn't dare delay rejuvenation until his new staff arrived that night. Odds were that he would have been fine, that no new danger would have threatened him in the meantime. But Jan was determined to make sure, rather than to trust the odds. He'd seen odds defied too many times. He'd done it himself.

The thought of his new staff brought to mind those who would no longer serve him—Herman, Ton, Roel. Their services would be missed. But only the loss of Marja stirred in him the faintest hint of remorse—which he quickly smothered. He'd witnessed the passing of too many years to dwell overly long on the death of any mortal.

An end table seemingly interposed itself where Jan was trying to step. He cracked his knee and cursed under his breath. He staggered onward. Between the various bullet wounds and his ankle, Jan was far from comfortable, but neither was he incapacitated. Or destroyed outright. He'd come out of the ambush by the Sabbat pack in better shape—that was, to say, with his head still attached to his torso—than he'd had a right to, considering his blunders.

I was so damned stupid!

As Jan limped across the living room and toward his own bedroom, shedding his bullet-riddled clothes and leaving them where they fell, he channeled his remaining energy away from invective and self-recrimination and to analysis of his mistakes. He'd made two. First, he'd failed to consider Baltimore itself a war zone. The city was his base of operations, but it was not a command center tucked far away from the hostilities. There was no such place left on the East Coast. The Sabbat, with the inroads they'd made, had seen to that. All that remained were a few scattered enclaves of Camarilla resistance: Baltimore, Buffalo, parts of New York City, the

Tremere chantry in the District of Columbia, Hartford.

My God, Jan thought. *How far we've fallen when Hartford is one of our places of power!*

The immensity of the task assigned him began, not for the first time, to overwhelm Jan. He was to wield the fractious elements of the Camarilla in the New World and prevent the Sabbat from gaining complete control of the East Coast, an undertaking that was already four-fifths accomplished.

Impossible.

Jan felt his resolve crumbling like an earthen damn eroded away over the years and pressed by the irresistible force of the ocean. He might plug a hole or two, or three, but did he possess enough fingers to make any real difference? Could he, or anyone, hold back the sea for long?

I must, he thought. *There is no alternative.* Hardestadt would allow no alternative.

Stripped naked, Jan made his way to the spacious lavatory. Ignoring the immense whirlpool tub, he climbed instead into the shower and turned the knob until the spray was scalding. The pinpricks of burning water stung the many bullet wounds, even partially healed over as they were. Jan welcomed the minor pain. It helped him focus his thoughts, enabled him to shunt aside the morbid defeatism that would be his doom, and concentrate again on his errors—errors he would be sure not to repeat.

It was true he had underestimated the danger in this city. He didn't fault himself, however, for the small retinue that he'd brought to the States. As he'd suspected it would be, the situation here was ticklish. Jan felt that he'd gained the upper hand over Victoria, and the cooperation of Prince Garlotte—both for the time being, at least. Whether or not he could have accomplished those goals if he'd brought a small army of personal retainers, if he'd been perceived as some imperial figure come to accept his coronation, was arguable at best. The others might well have banded together against him, as they still might. But having now established himself as a leader of the Camarilla resistance, Jan would take that chance rather than skimp on security in the future.

The actual mistake, he realized, was not in his choice of retinue but in the decision to venture out into the city. The desire to get away from the Lord Baltimore Inn, to get away more specifically from Victoria, had been so strong. *And so I abandoned the one place in the city I knew to be safe haven—or relatively safe*, he corrected himself, remembering the reports of the destruction of Maria Chin, the initial Tremere representative to the "conference." Victoria had been involved in the attack on Chin as well, he recalled. The Tremere had been coming to meet Victoria. Jan filed away that thought for closer examination later.

His own second mistake, which had greatly compounded the first, was that, consumed by the considerable political and martial necessities, he'd neglected personal necessities. In particular, he'd allowed his strength to wane. He'd waited too long between feedings. The lapse was understandable, but no more acceptable.

What will Hardestadt say if he finds out? Jan wondered, but he didn't really want to consider that possibility. His sire might feign indifference, but the inevitable off-hand yet skillfully barbed comments would begin, and a thinly veiled word of censure from Hardestadt would pain Jan more than a stake through the heart. And that would be only the beginning. Jan might never know for certain if, through incompetence, he'd forfeited the favor of his sire, and if that incompetence was compounded by failure...

Jan had seen others of his brethren fallen from grace. They might linger for decades, wondering, not knowing how significantly they'd offended their sire, but at some point, the vitae—the gift and the curse—was reclaimed. The end, Jan suspected, was not as bad as the years of doubt preceding it. He did not intend to find out.

There had been so much to do before and upon his arrival in Baltimore, so many individuals to be contacted in the space of a very few nights: Colchester, Xaviar the Gangrel justicar, the Giovanni in Boston, the various princes, agents in Chicago. All of those preparations, however, would go for naught if he, through carelessness or neglect, were destroyed. As it was, he had almost been too weak to prevail over the Sabbat assassins.

Not almost, he corrected himself. *I was too weak. If it weren't for Bell, I would be destroyed and Blaine would be walking about, instead of the other way around.*

Jan and Blaine had been acquaintances, if not friends, long ago. Jan didn't know what had led to the *antitribu's* decision to abandon his clan in favor of the Sabbat, and Jan didn't particularly care. Blaine had always been of a coarser weave. He was a social inferior even before turning traitor, and now he was destroyed. Case closed.

Theo Bell was a more pertinent enigma. He had rescued Jan, but that didn't explain why the Brujah was there in the first place. Coincidence? *Possible,* Jan thought, *but doubtful.* Coincidence, Jan had come to realize over the years, was generally the least likely explanation for any occurrence. There were always hidden plans behind the obvious schemes, and often other forces behind the hidden plans. Jan was no stranger to the halls of Kindred power; his lineage had seen to that. But among his own machinations, he was often left ignorant of the designs of Hardestadt, he who was so close to the maneuverings of members of the Inner Circle. And at times, Jan had come to believe that other, more mysterious powers were pulling strings—strings that even venerable Hardestadt, though he might know of their existence, could not control.

Old wives' tales, Jan chided himself. *Almost as fanciful as stones of the Antediluvians.* The elders of the Camarilla had wisely pronounced such stories to be fiction, yet so many Kindred failed to appreciate the mythic nature of the legends. Adam and Eve, the Garden of Eden, Caine and Abel—such myths addressed certain metaphysical themes, but among the masses of the less erudite, many took the stories as history.

Jan paused in his rumination. Something smooth pressed against his face. White tile. He was leaning forward against the wall of the tiled shower, much of his weight supported by his face as his mind wandered. Jan pushed himself upright, turned off the water. He'd neglected to close the shower door, and a pool of tepid water had spread across the floor. Steam hung thick and heavy in the air, obscuring the far side of the room. Jan stepped carefully as he walked across the water into nothingness.

Billows of steam fled before him when he opened the door into the bedroom. He grabbed one of the plush towels from the bathroom and dried himself, slowly, luxuriously. The air conditioner was on high, and the sharp chill made his skin draw tight after the steam from the shower. He banished all extraneous thought. His mind and body were too tired. Wandering thoughts were a waste of time and symptomatic of a lack of discipline. Methodically he inspected each inch of his body, noted each bullet wound and estimated how much blood would be required to heal it. He tested his weight on his ankle, only briefly, before deciding that substantial repair would have to wait for another night. But he would not continue in this weakened state. Not even for another hour.

A great lethargy pulled at him, above and beyond the weariness brought on by his injuries. Outside, the sun would soon rise. Heavy shields were drawn across all the windows in the suite, but still Jan knew. He forced himself to disregard the lullaby of dawn and, with deliberate motions, dressed in loose, gray satin garments that would shortly serve as pajamas. He moved barefoot into the living room, where a disheveled man— his nametag read *Jeffrey Taylor*—sat with his face in his hands.

Jan moved closer, stood over the man whose inn uniform seemed an out-of-place prop. The assistant night manager—any employee of this inn, for that matter—normally displayed a sunny disposition for guests, but this man sobbed and dug the tips of his fingers into his face and scalp. Jan noticed again the thick comfort of the elegant carpet against the skin of his ever-cold feet. His senses had jumped into the hyper-aware state that accompanied the expectation of feeding.

"Jeffrey," said Jan quietly. The man looked up only reluctantly. His eyes, bloodshot pools, reflected the anguish that wracked his body and soul. Jan's voice, though, soothed the man slightly. "Jeffrey, what is her name?"

He opened his mouth, but a new spasm of sobbing took him before he could speak. Jan waited patiently, allowing his comforting presence to tame the man's hysteria.

"Jeffrey?"

"Her name is…Estelle," he managed to choke out.

Estelle. Jan held the name in his mind. It would make his task easier, though knowing her name caused him unease as well. *Estelle.* She was now that much more of a person. Her name was one more facet to the generic desk attendant. *Estelle.*

"Jeffrey," Jan placed his hand on the man's forehead, "Estelle is working a double shift. She will not be going home. Call whomever needs to know." Jan paused, waited for the instructions to take hold, but did not release the assistant night manager. "You do not feel well, Jeffrey. Go home. Remember none of this. Do you understand?"

Jeffrey nodded weakly. He took a deep breath and stood. "Is... is there anything else I can help you with, Mr. Pieterzoon?"

"No. Thank you, Jeffrey." Jan placed his hand on Jeffrey's cheek. "Take care of yourself."

"Yes. I...I will." He took another deep breath and moved to the door, a thick fog clearing only slowly from his mind. "Thank you, Mr. Pieterzoon." Jan allowed thoughts of the mortal to drift away. Jeffrey Taylor would make the phone call and then go home. He would be fine by tomorrow night, except never again would he be comfortable in the presence of a certain front-desk attendant. Around her, he would experience an unsettling sense of guilt—for what, he'd have no idea. He would avoid her, and when he couldn't avoid her, he'd deal with the discomfort. But he would live.

Jan turned and strode slowly, purposefully, to the double doors he'd attempted, less than an hour ago, to pretend did not exist. He turned the knob and stepped into the bedroom. *Estelle.*

She lay crumpled on the bed, her small body dwarfed by the king-sized expanse. The silk necktie, a makeshift gag, was wet with her saliva and tears. Her hands were tied behind her, her clothes torn aside. She cried quietly into the bedspread. *Estelle.*

Jan forced himself to look at her, not to avert his eyes. *You are the cause of this,* he told himself. *Make no mistake.* He was speaking to her before he reached the bed, before he knelt gently at her side. "Estelle..."

He untied her wrists, noticed the abrasions from her struggle against the drapery cords. "Estelle," he shushed her sobs, as he removed the tie from her mouth. She sucked in air, pressed her face against Jan's knee. He was her protector, her salvation. His voice was a salve to her injury. "Estelle, it's not your fault."

It's my fault, he knew, but he smothered the guilt in pity. He straightened her clothing while she clung whimpering to his arm—eased her skirt back into place, hooked her brassiere, buttoned what buttons had not been ripped from her shirt. He pretended that he was her rescuer—as she believed—rather than the inhuman beast that had set all this in motion. He held her head against his chest, stroked her hair. He wished that her tears plastering his shirt against his skin were, instead, a knife that could carve out his black heart. In a way, they were.

Jan preferred to come along after the fact—*long* after the fact. Then the lion's share of the harm was already done, and he merely took advantage in his own, lesser way. But circumstances could be cruel. There was not always the luxury of finding a Marja or a Roel. The shelters, many of which Jan supported financially, were not always convenient. Sometimes he had to start from scratch, and he could not hide from himself the monster he'd become.

"Estelle," he whispered again, soothing her even as he pierced the flesh of her neck. *No*, he told himself, as he thought of the rapists, *I am no better.* In the best of cases, he took advantage of the victim; in the worst of cases, such as tonight, he created the victim.

I am no better.

Estelle pressed against him like a frightened child and slept. Her racing heart, a ceaseless accusation, hammered in his ears. Jan could feel the pull of the sun beyond the light-sealed walls, but it was many hours before he surrendered to the day.

Monday, 19 July 1999, 10:16 PM
Governor's Suite, Lord Baltimore Inn
Baltimore, Maryland

"Really, Alexander, I can't see why you refuse me this!" Victoria was well beyond pouting and footstomping, and was working herself into a full-fledged rage. A single lock of her perfect, dark-brown hair fell out of place across her forehead. She brushed it aside irritably.

Prince Garlotte stood and watched her tantrum brewing. His childe, Isaac, likewise stood—Victoria had not offered them a seat, though, in the larger sense, she was the guest. The young sheriff looked on and tried not to squirm as the Toreador insulted his sire. For what else could it be but an insult to give the prince an ultimatum, and then spurn his hospitality when he refused to comply? Two of Gainesmil's underlings scurried about packing Victoria's belongings—belongings that, almost to the last gown, were gifts from the prince. Added insult.

"You know," said Garlotte, "how it pains me to refuse you anything, my love."

"Then don't refuse me," she snapped.

"Ah, Victoria." The prince reached out to lay a hand on her arm, but she withdrew, gracefully yet pointedly, from his reach. He watched her brush the lock of hair away from her face again. *How perfectly you've choreographed it all, Victoria,* he thought, *down to the last curl. My God, she's lovely with that fire in her eyes!* As she turned her back to him, Garlotte noticed Isaac cringing at the slight, but the prince was too captivated by the curve of Victoria's spine, the perfect flare of her hips, to be insulted.

She faced the prince again and began to speak, but paused and looked at Isaac, as she had earlier.

"I assure you," said Garlotte, "you may speak freely before Isaac. He is the model of discretion." The prince noted with pride as his childe very nearly succeeded in disguising a flinch. *He's learning. Give him a few more decades....*

"My most earnest desire is to protect you, my prince," she said at last, a forced calm blunting her rage.

"Of course it is, my dear."

Victoria planted her fists on her hips. "So I tell you again: You must send Jan away."

"And I ask you again," said the prince. "Why?" Victoria's brief show of patience came to an abrupt end. She flashed a glare at Garlotte and Isaac that would have brought a mortal to his knees. As it was, Isaac took a step back.

"He plots to take your city."

Garlotte let her accusation linger between them...before he dismissed it. "But Isaac and I have just come from inspecting some of the city's defenses—manned by Kindred newly arrived from Chicago, as a favor to Jan."

"Not as a favor to Jan," Victoria corrected the prince. "As a favor to his bloodthirsty sire."

"Who among us is *not* bloodthirsty?" Garlotte asked in feigned innocence.

Victoria, exasperated, turned toward the open French doors and the balcony. "Don't be dense, Alexander. Certainly he protects the physical security of the city. Another Sabbat pit is of no value to him. He will maneuver you from power."

"He has told you this?" Garlotte asked her.

Victoria ignored the prince's preposterous suggestion and turned her wrath instead upon the two skulking Toreador who carted load after load of her finery out of the inn. "Leave us! I came to this city penniless. I can do without whatever is left. Wait for me at the truck."

As the two lesser Toreador scampered away, Garlotte could not deny two implications of their presence, one for each underling. First, Gainesmil had chosen sides in this matter, or at the very least he'd ingratiated himself to Victoria. *But can*

I begrudge him the desire to be close to her? Garlotte wondered. He pondered the question for a few seconds before reaching a conclusion: *Absolutely.* Gainesmil would be brought to heel. Garlotte would make sure that the architect came to see the error of his ways.

Second, considering that the movers had arrived almost simultaneously with Garlotte and Isaac, Victoria must have held out little or no hope that she would sway the prince. *But why create an open break?* Garlotte wondered as he stroked his dark beard. *Is she playing to my sense of chivalry? Does she expect I'll try to win her back?* He had no conclusive evidence, but of one thing the prince was certain: Even Victoria's most capricious whim was driven by devious, inscrutable purpose. And tonight that purpose pulled her away from him.

"I cannot remain your guest and watch you destroyed," Victoria said.

Garlotte said nothing. He merely gazed at her—at the strong and gracious lines of her face, the weave of the white sweater as it lay upon her breasts, the golden locket that he had given her.

I can let her go, the prince told himself, and though it was true, the fact that he could did not mean that he *wanted,* to do so.

"The conference won't stand for his heavy-handed ways," Victoria continued. "With time for a little reflection before the next meeting, they'll see him for the usurper he is."

With *a little reflection and a hit of persuasion…* Garlotte interpreted her comment, but he had not overlooked the potential threat of the displaced masses. "There is no more conference."

Victoria glared at him, the challenge obvious in her eyes. *Did she really think I'd allow the rabble to influence policy once some semblance of stability was restored?* Garlotte wondered. Had he overestimated Victoria, or was her apparent outrage merely another feint?

"The majority of refugees have been assigned duties upholding the city's defenses," he explained. "There is no longer any need to consult them in matters of planning. *They,* Victoria, realize that a strong city, shelter against the Sabbat, is the most they should hope for. They did not enjoy free rein in their old cities. Nor should they expect it here."

"I see." Victoria's hand rose slowly to the locket. Her gaze shifted and came to rest on Isaac. For a long moment she studied him, but then her interest in him seemed to dissipate instantly.

"But there's no need for you to leave," Garlotte suggested.

Victoria turned back to Garlotte. She tugged at the locket with just enough force that the thin chain tore apart behind her neck. As if to punctuate her rejection of Garlotte, she set locket and chain on the table before him, then left without another word.

Prince Garlotte closed his eyes and savored the last traces of her lingering scent. He wanted to imprint the memory of her on his mind's eye, so that she would ever be there beside him. For a fleeting moment, the world receded, and there was only she and he, until...

"Should I follow her?" Isaac's voice shattered the illusion.

Garlotte fought down the deep growl that began in his belly. "Follow her? To Gainesmil's haven? I believe I know where to find it." The prince's tone precluded further questions.

He took his late wife's locket, that piece of jewelry that had until moments ago rested against Victoria's chest, from the table. The chain could be repaired easily enough. Garlotte's eyebrow rose with interest, however, when he opened the locket and found the shriveled tongue resting within.

I determine my own destiny, Victoria reassured herself. The limousine that Gainesmil had sent carried her gently over the city streets and followed behind the truck full of her possessions. Her hand strayed to her throat, to the space where the chain no longer rested. She'd given it back to Garlotte, and along with it the memento of her time with the fiend Elford in Atlanta.

They don't think I mean business. Alexander, Jan, Theo Bell, Vitel, the new Tremere witch—none of them took Victoria seriously. Elford had made that same mistake. His gnarled tongue was a warning. *Let Garlotte understand, if he has eyes to see,* she thought, then, *He won't understand. Not until it's too late.*

The prince was not wrong to be suspicious of Victoria, but if he trusted Jan, he was a fool. And he would suffer the consequences. Either Jan would depose Garlotte, or Victoria might be driven to it herself. But that would be many weeks or months down the road. Tonight, she had set a more immediate gambit in motion. Garlotte might think that he could do without her company, but let him try. Then add to that another factor: Without Victoria actively opposing Jan, Garlotte would have much less reason to support his clanmate. She had planted the seed in the prince's mind that Jan was a threat. Garlotte would also likely blame Jan's presence for the estrangement between herself and the prince.

We'll see how long before cracks form in the Ventrue good-old-boys network, she thought.

But it wasn't Garlotte, or even Jan, that Victoria feared. She still could not shake the feeling that she was merely playing an assigned role in this drama. That was her greatest and constant fear, and she'd taken steps, again, to see that it was not borne out.

He brought his childe. The prince had responded to Victoria's summons—her *invitation*, rather—but he had brought Isaac with him. So Victoria had left. She had aligned herself, to a certain degree at least, against the prince. Had he come alone, she would have allowed herself to be talked into staying. She would have sent Gainesmil's underlings away without her in the end. She would have abandoned this latest plan. She was determined, above all else, that no elder being would out-guess her. Not every time.

Yet the feeling that she sleepwalked through someone else's dream clung to her like a fever, as it had increasingly since Atlanta. As it had since her time in the clutches of the vile Tzimisce. Now Victoria's fingers brushed the tiny imperfection on her jaw—the image of a serpent swallowing its own tail— that her makeup seemed capable of hiding for only so long.

I determine my own destiny, she told herself, over and over again, as the limousine passed farther into the night.

Prince Garlotte already had sent Isaac away to inspect more of the city's defenses. Now the prince reclined on the couch and pretended that Victoria was still there. It was much easier without his childe babbling on about nothing. Garlotte imagined that the impression of her body was still warm—the way her body had been warm that night on the ship—on the cushions beneath him, or on the bed in the other room. He tried to convince himself that he could still catch a hint of her fragrance. He considered keeping the belongings she'd left behind—aside from the decomposing tongue on the coffee table, of course—and going on as if she resided permanently in his inn. He could seal the suite, so no one would ever disturb the space she had inhabited.

My God, he sighed. He had not anticipated the ache that had gripped him after not even a full hour of her absence. It wasn't that he had to be with her every moment. Over the past few weeks, in fact, he'd spent relatively little time in her actual presence. To know that he *could* be with her, that she was at his beck and call, was enough; to know that he could not see her, that she would turn him away…that might well drive him to distraction.

Ah, well, he tried to resign himself, *I might need a bit of distraction.*

"What do you think?" Garlotte said to the empty room.

"I was waiting for her to flash some titty," came the reply. "I figure she's enough woman for you and junior—and me, I'm okay with watching."

Garlotte sat up and faced the Nosferatu. Colchester rubbed his hands together and stared into the distance, as if replaying in his mind what hadn't happened. "I would think," the prince admonished him, "that you'd have tired of playing peeping tom by now."

Colchester wheezed and…grinned? It was hard to tell with the fangs jutting through his lip. "Mostly, yeah. But she's enough to put starch back in your collar."

Garlotte frowned. He did not care to hear Victoria spoken of in so coarse a manner. Colchester apparently realized his mistake; his manner sobered rather abruptly.

Garlotte pressed on. "And she and Pieterzoon have not… *encountered* one another again since what you reported two nights ago?"

"That's right."

Colchester's perverse glee having faded, Garlotte could read nothing at all in the solid black eyes, the cratered face. *I would have done better not to have put him on his guard*, the prince thought, but the Nosferatu's lechery grated so, to an irrational extent. *Some matters*, Garlotte decided, reaffirming his own actions, *aren't meant to be rational.*

Thursday, 22 July 1999, 4:31 AM
A subterranean grotto
New York City, New York

Calebros shifted in the desk chair. It was so difficult to find a comfortable seat, considering the peculiar curvature of his spine. He returned a sheet of paper—a brief report noting his suspicions about a certain Setite; Calebros had added a comment about another Tremere assassination in Baltimore, the Setite's base of operations—to one of the precarious stacks of books and folders on his battered, overcrowded desk.

He skimmed another report—the latest from Washington—then turned and fed a scrap of brown paper bag into his typewriter.

IMAGE 2

22 July 1999
Re: Baltimore/Washington D.C.,

Courier reports——according to
Ravenna/Parmenides, no Sabbat plans for
imminent attack on Baltimore; slow
build-up/organization/consolidation
continues; no sign shift of forces
north, i.e., Buffalo.

Colchester to keep Garlotte,
Pieterzoon informed of info from
R/P re: D.C.

Pieterzoon not aware
of Colchester dealings
w/ Garlotte.

Keep it that way.

Tuesday, July 27 1999, 3:16 AM
Chantry of the Five Boroughs
New York City, New York

"All of them, *Regentia*?" the overwhelmed novice asked. "All of them," Sturbridge replied. "And I want all of his papers: his notes, his letters, his grocery lists for that matter. All of these books that are not in their proper places, I want them. If they are lying open, mark the pages. If they're not open, scan them for marginalia and mark those pages.

"Give the whole room—make that the room and the entire way down to the Exeunt Tercius—a good going-over for any resonances. Anything you find, I want that too. That ought to get me started. What do you know about the ritual he was enacting when he was...interrupted?"

The novice's eyes kept involuntarily straying to the drained, crumpled body at the room's center. "I don't...I mean, it's a Questing obviously, looking at the *diagrama hermetica* but... Surely Jacqueline would be better able to answer these questions. She assisted in preparing for..." The novice broke off, but recovered herself quickly. "I'll send her along too," she added hastily, forestalling the next order.

Sturbridge paused, then dropped the finger that was raised to instruct Eva on this very point. She smiled. "Better. Tell me, how would you say he died?"

"Something went wrong, *Regentia*. The protective circle has been effaced in places, the candles overturned. We're lucky the whole room didn't go up in flames...."

"It can't, but go on," Sturbridge interjected.

Eva looked questioningly at the Regent, but as no further

information seemed forthcoming, she continued her speculation. "The ritual went wrong. Something...stepped through. It killed him, claimed his vitae, and fled. That way, towards the Exeunt Tercius and out. Aaron tried to block its escape and was killed as well."

Sturbridge shook her head slowly. "You're rushing ahead. But perhaps you do not appreciate the danger. We're dealing with death here—the Final Death. Do you understand? When you hunt mortals, you can be ravenous. If you would contest with Death, however, you must be dispassionate. You must be disciplined. You must be patient. Death is so very...patient."

She drew out the last word like a caress. But there was no warmth in it. "You proceed from too many assumptions. For starters, how did the ritual go wrong? Foley was an *adeptus*. He was assisted by two apprentices, one of the third circle, one of the seventh circle, either of whom could have pulled off a simple Questing by her- or himself. It simply does not hold together."

Eva began to protest, but was cut off.

"Two. You can't 'step through' a Questing. Nor can any of the denizens from the 'other side'. That's an old wives' tale, fit only for frightening neophytes. A Questing is not like throwing wide the postern gate. It's more like putting an eye to the keyhole. A seeing, rather than a going. Or, as a *diligent* novice would say, a scrying rather than..."

"An apportation," Eva finished quickly, ducking the rather longish lecture implicit in the Regent's glare. "But what if it wasn't just a Questing? What if it was a full-blown Summoning? I know the standard precautions aren't in place—there are none of the names of the archangelic protectors, no warding of the cardinal points, nothing more efficacious than chalk and candlelight and quill and parchment. But maybe he didn't want anyone to *know* it was a Summoning."

The Regent gave her a look of stern reproach. "You know full well that it is forbidden to perform any Summoning within the *domicilia*. To even assist in such an ill-conceived venture would be to invite my extreme displeasure."

The tone of this last pronouncement carried a far greater threat than the words themselves. Eva, however, was too caught up in fitting together the pieces of her theory to take the hint. "All the more reason for him to conceal the true nature of the ritual! Any of the protective *diagrama* would have given him away. His assistants would have divined his purpose and," she paused triumphantly and then suddenly remembered herself. "And dissuaded him from such a disobedient course of action," she finished somewhat lamely.

"Yes, the assistants, " Sturbridge resumed the narrative. "Who Foley had decided to include in his 'secret' ritual for what purpose? It seems to me that not even Druids, Satanists and Templars go to such great lengths to ensure that their secret rites are so well-attended."

"If I might speak frankly, *Regentia,*" Eva began meekly, "There are those within our chantry who do not feel as fervently about the *interdicti* as you and I do."

Sturbridge raised herself up to her full height and seemed for a moment as if she might strike the novice. Eva, for her part, scrutinized some detail of the complex pattern of floor tiles, her head bent in submission.

Sturbridge exhaled audibly. "The *interdicti* exist precisely to keep foolish novices from indulging their folly unto self-destruction.

"Whether you realize it or not," the Regent pressed on, "we are besieged here. Do you know what lies beyond these walls?"

A slight smile stole over Eva's features before she could suppress it. She was thinking about the relatively cloistered campus of Barnard College upon which the chantry was situated. She wisely did not give voice to these thoughts.

"Beyond these walls," Sturbridge continued, "lies enemy territory. New York is a Sabbat stronghold. *The* Sabbat stronghold. Thus far, you have been carefully shielded from this harsh and uncompromising reality. But surely even from within the safety of this chantry, you realize what is at stake here."

"Yes, Regentia." Eva's tone was submissive.

Sturbridge raised the novice's downcast face. "We can hold the ravening Sabbat at bay. We *will* hold them at bay. But we will do it the right way. We will not resort to high-risk rituals—especially those that dispense with proper wardings—within the confines of the chantry. We will not endanger our sisters in our search for better weapons to bring to bear upon our enemies. We will not embroil other powers—particularly those from beyond this terrestrial sphere—in our struggle.

"What is most important in fighting monsters is to ensure that one does not..."

"Become a monster," Eva finished quoting the philosopher. Nietzsche was a countryman of hers, part of the complex intellectual and mystic tradition that was her birthright. Eva could not help but call to mind, however, that the words of the philosopher were also part of the birthright of the Reich. How often were his aphorisms used to defend and expound a pogrom of genocide that humbled even the worst excesses of the undying?

Words too, it seemed, could become desperate and monstrous.

Sturbridge put a hand on the novice's shoulder and steered her towards the doorway. "But you look weary. Go to the refectory. Get some nourishment into your system. Then—and only then—may you return here and gather the things I have requested." As Sturbridge closed the chamber door behind them, Eva visibly sagged, as if the immediacy of the corpse was the only thing that had been keeping her upright. She staggered down the corridor toward the refectory. A somnambulist. Sturbridge watched the receding figure until it reached the bend in the passage, as if to make certain that it would not stumble and fall before then. Satisfied, she called after her, "Eva..."

The figure turned with apparent effort.

"Be wary. Not all monsters come from beyond these walls."

Sturbridge strode off purposefully towards her sanctum. The few novices she passed along the way, catching sight of their Regent's demeanor, pressed back into doorways and side corridors to let her pass.

Sturbridge batted absently at something before her face as if trying to clear away a cobweb or persistent insect. She purposefully triggered no fewer than three defensive systems (two silent and one very much audible) which she left for the security team to disarm in her wake. She was none too pleased with the demonstration of their obvious shortcomings two nights earlier and was not inclined to make their work any more enjoyable tonight.

She even went so far as to collar a particularly perverse guardian spirit and dispatch it to convince the chantry's autonomic defenses that the *domicilia* was ablaze. That particular impossibility ought to keep them occupied for some time. They would probably have to take the "malfunctioning" system offline, dismantling the complex series of mystic, electronic, biochemical and geomechanical wardings one by one.

It was, perhaps, a small cruelty. But not one which Sturbridge repented. The punishment was, if anything, overly lenient compared to the bloodprice she might have exacted for the failure two night's past—a failure that had resulted in the murder of her second-in-command in the sanctuary of his own workshop.

As she passed into her own sanctum, she noted with satisfaction that the door sealed itself behind her with the hiss of hydraulics and the singing of steel bolts ramming home. She called for the status of the chantry's exits and found them all secured. She crossed to the desk and keyed a gimel-level override, unbarring one of the exits (the Exeunt Tercius, just to rub their noses in it a bit). A few quick gestures and she set a ward—a screamer, and a loud one—to go off when the door was resecured, crying the exact response time.

Only then did she allow herself to collapse into the overstuffed armchair in the room's farthest corner. This chair was the only concession to comfort in the austere study. Even so, there was something imposing, almost throne-like, about it.

The chair seemed to rise from a dais of piled books. Jumbled stacks of tomes rose to well above shoulder-level in places, swaying precariously. Not infrequently, an entire wing of the edifice would break away and cascade to the floor in an avalanche of illuminated manuscripts, fashion magazines, papyrus scrolls, advertising circulars, penciled manuscripts, clay tablets and loose-leaf paper.

Safely ensconced, Sturbridge was finally able to ignore the dark shapes that fluttered in her peripheral vision and demanded attention. Instead, she focused upon thoughts of Eva and, more specifically, the faulty theory the girl had hastily constructed. Johnston Foley not had gone to Final Death at the whim of a beast of spirit—the preparations for his ritual were all wrong. Rather, he'd met destruction at the hand (and blade) of a beast of flesh, undead flesh. The killer had indeed, as Eva hypothesized, claimed Foley's vitae, but he'd taken something else as well—a certain gem that had been the subject of Foley's ritual. This was where Sturbridge held a distinct advantage over poor Eva. The regent had access to much more data. She was aware of so much more—such as a disturbing pattern of murders perpetrated against Clan Tremere, a pattern into which Foley's demise fit all too well.

Oppressed by morbid thoughts and by the black fluttering that again closed around her, Sturbridge sank more deeply into her voluminous chair. She wrapped herself in the enfolding wall of books, pulling it tightly about her. She felt its reassuring proximity, its warmth, its protection. Slowly, the dark wings that buffeted about her face began to recede.

She was more than casually acquainted with their shadowy touch—the flurry of blows that neither cut nor bruised but rather seemed to smother. Her ears rang with the cry of carrion birds. She could feel their weight above her, hovering oppressively like the noonday sun, waiting. One among them, bolder than its fellows, picked experimentally at the hem of one sleeve.

She snatched back her hand to within the shelter of the cocoon of books. Her first instinct was to lash out, to strike, to shriek, to frighten and scatter the murder of crows. With effort, she suppressed this instinctive animal response.

She knew better. There was no point in expending her energies in avenging herself upon mere messengers, upon these harbingers of the end. She withheld her scorn, reserved it for their master, the one true nemesis.

So he was come among them once again. Sturbridge found herself unconsciously gathering her defenses about her, sketching the outlines of cunning wards, beckoning to unseen allies. She harbored no illusion as to the eventual outcome of the life-long confrontation. Even her (not inconsiderable) powers would avail little against her unwelcome guest. Sturbridge was no legendary beauty, to compel suitors and rivals to overcome intervening oceans and generations. Her suitor, however, possessed an inhuman patience and persistence.

It was not the first time that Death had come to call upon her. She only hoped that, this time, he would not be inclined to linger.

Wednesday, 28 July 1999, 11:09 PM
Presidential Suite, Lord Baltimore Inn
Baltimore, Maryland

"Any more Sabbat incursions near the city?" Jan asked.
"No," answered Hans van Pel, Jan's current assistant, in crisp, clipped English. As always, he carried a small pad of paper and a pen, but Jan had never seen the man take notes. Which was just as well, since written records were more vulnerable to destruction or theft. Hans stored a multitudinous array of facts in his mind and exercised infallible recall. "There have been minor probes, but none have progressed past the outer perimeter that Mr. Bell has established near Fort Meade."

Jan nodded. The effectiveness of Bell's perimeter was aided immensely by the sudden spate of construction along massive swaths of northbound I-95, the Gladys Spellman Parkway, and other major arteries of traffic from Washington. Garlotte, via several government officials within his considerable sphere of influence, had had no trouble arranging for the overly ambitious projects by the Department of Transportation. Snarled, one-lane, bumper-to-bumper traffic was relatively easy to monitor, and from the mortal viewpoint, there was nothing unusual about the D.O.T. closing and tearing up miles and miles of road more than it could ever work on at one time. "And the inner lines are prepared?"

"Yes. The second line at Baltimore-Washington International Airport, the third along the perimeter highway, and the fourth at the city limits are all as secure as possible."

Jan began to slide through his fingers two of the bullets that had been lodged in his body and which had popped out when the wounds healed. His assistant did his best to ignore the grating sound of the metal slugs.

"Speaking of Mr. Bell," van Pel continued, "the increased resistance he met on his latest raid into Washington suggests that the Sabbat forces are consolidating."

"Which seems to corroborate information from our source within the Sabbat high command that they are massing for an all-out assault on Baltimore." Jan caressed the smooth surface of the bullets, slid them over one finger, under the next.

A slight frown crept over Hans's features at mention of the mysterious informant. "Are you confident of the veracity of your source, sir?"

Jan's gaze focused on his assistant. "No." Colchester, on the first night they had met, had briefed Jan about the assassin faux-ghoul who served the Lady Sascha Vykos but still reported to his Assamite masters via the Nosferatu. Jan was suspicious of the chain of information; not that Colchester would mislead him, but there were too many links, too many possible ulterior motives. If the information from that source, however, was confirmed by other reports...

"Bell's losses on the raid were relatively light," said van Pel. "And they were all Brujah, at any rate.

We'll need all those Brujah when the time comes." Jan was amazed that Bell managed to withdraw from Washington with *any* of his forces. Several times, he'd pressed well within the Beltway and fought his way back out. Some losses were unavoidable, and Jan knew that he might as well try to bottle a hurricane as control the Brujah archon.

"And the refugee corps?" Jan asked.

"As Prince Garlotte decreed, the majority of those Kindred seeking shelter in Baltimore have been pressed into service—the price of sanctuary. The sheriff and Gainesmil have formed them into units, and they man the checkpoints along the inner perimeters. The Brujah and our friends from Chicago have been assigned the more sensitive and vital areas."

"Good." As the bullets clicked among his fingers, Jan could not chase a nagging thought from his mind. "Why attack Baltimore first?" he muttered to himself.

"Sir?"

"Why attack Baltimore first," Jan repeated, his gaze focused on some indeterminate point in the mid distance, "when they still have to worry about other points: Buffalo, New York City, Hartford? New York is too strong, of course, but why not pick off the others, then bring their full weight to bear on Baltimore, then New York? That's what I'd do."

"They didn't have much trouble so far just marching up the coast," van Pel suggested.

"But none of the princes were expecting such massive assaults. We've had time to fortify now, while the Sabbat consolidated its gains."

"Perhaps," said Hans, "they'd rather attack the defenses here than face the Gangrel at Buffalo."

"Possible." Jan removed his glasses and rubbed the tiny red marks on his nose. "And Xaviar might be close enough to support Hartford if it were attacked."

Talk of Hartford raised other concerns in Jan's mind. His overtures to the Giovanni in Boston had met with lukewarm response. Representatives of that incestuous clan were willing enough to talk with him, but with the outcome of the East Coast war so definitely up in the air, they were quite unwilling to support the Camarilla. Granted, the Giovanni refusals were couched in such diplomatic language as to seem practically to agree with Jan's requests. But they would not endanger themselves for the Camarilla. They had not survived as an independent clan for so long by choosing sides. *If it comes to it,* Jan thought, *I might have to point out to them that, eventually, not to choose the Camarilla is to choose the Sabbat. If they're not with us...*

"Sir, is there anything else?"

Jan waved away his assistant. "Inform Baas that I am not to be disturbed for the rest of the night, unless the prince or Archon Bell call."

With that, Hans van Pel, efficient to a fault, was gone. The full weight of ominous responsibility was upon Jan again, and he had no desire to discuss more details unless absolutely necessary. Baas, the head of security now that Herman and Ton were dead, would see to Jan's privacy. The replacement entourage had been in place for over a week. In addition to van Pel, there were four clerks; all five satisfied Jan's dietary needs. And, of course, there was Anton Baas and the fifteen members of his security team. Prince Garlotte had not gone so far as to say anything about the additional armed presence. How could he, after Jan briefed him in detail regarding the assassination attempt? But the number of the prince's guards on the premises of the inn had conspicuously increased as well—response to the attack on Jan, or to Jan's additional personnel?

Surely Garlotte can't believe that I present a threat to him, or that I want to take his city, Jan thought. Although, the more he thought about it, the more wistful he grew. The trials of a prince, of ruling over a single city, would be child's play compared to the burden Hardestadt had laid on Jan's shoulders: dealing with various princes, each habitually consumed by his own needs and desires; trying to keep abreast of the secretive activities of Clan Tremere, which had seemed strangely passive through the crisis thus far; puzzling out the motives driving certain loose cannons, like Theo Bell and Victoria.

The mere thought of Victoria made Jan's chest involuntarily constrict. He couldn't help but picture his hands on her slim waist. He saw the pain and fear in her eyes when he'd noticed the mark on her jaw.

She is marked by the Tzimisce, he thought. *Is she their pawn?* He couldn't be sure—Colchester had watched her for a few nights, but there was too much to be done elsewhere—but the mere suspicion was excuse enough for him to stay away from her, to keep sufficient distance between them so that he didn't have to contend with urges he hadn't felt since…since many years ago and his turbulent relationship with Lucita.

Lucita. There was a name Jan had long since hardened his heart against. Victoria was infinitely more vulnerable than Lucita. Besides *wanting* Victoria, he wanted to protect her, to watch over her. These emotions that Victoria evoked were different from what he'd felt for Lucita, but similar in that Jan didn't want to feel any of them. Eternal existence was fraught with enough pain and disappointment without the additional inconvenience of such sentimental weaknesses, which were more the hallmark of mortals.

Jan's suspicion of Victoria, the fact that she might somehow, with or without her knowledge, be under the sway of the Sabbat, was justification for avoiding her altogether. Victoria's having moved out of the inn a week and a half ago made the task of avoiding her that much easier. Since the attack, Jan had kept to the inn and under the close eye of Baas and his security brigade. Jan hated to think how difficult that confinement could have been, how disconcerting to have known that Victoria was just at the other end of a long corridor. But, thankfully, she had left. She and Gariotte had argued about something, and she had stormed out to set up house with Robert Gainesmil. Jan wasn't sure whether to be grateful to or envious of the Toreador architect who had inherited Victoria's proximity.

More consequential, however, were the implications of her departure's timing. She had left the night after the assassination attempt on Jan. *Is there a connection?* he wondered. His suspicions rose to fill every crevice of doubt, but was this justified, or merely his own attempt to crowd out any other feelings he harbored for Victoria? He couldn't be sure. He seemed incapable of purely rational thought where this woman was concerned.

Better not to think of her at all.

Jan rose to his feet and was relieved in a way when the stiffness and ragged pain of his ankle suddenly consumed his thoughts. He'd fed repeatedly since his new entourage had arrived from Amsterdam, but it was simply not feasible for him to consume the amount of blood required to make him whole. Besides, there was no time for the surgery required—that would *still* be required at some point—to align properly his broken bones. So for now, he hobbled. The first few steps were always the worst, or if he remained on his feet for very long at a stretch the pain became disagreeable. At times like this, however, when certain thoughts dogged him, thoughts he didn't want to face, Jan found the distraction useful.

He hobbled to the door of the smallest of the bedrooms attached to the suite. "Estelle," he said quietly as he entered.

She didn't lift her head, but he knew that she heard him. Her dark, shoulder-length hair was lustrous in the sparse light. Jan

had washed her hair, had washed her, with warm soapy water
and a soft washcloth, just last night. He had caressed her body
with expensive lotions. Their subtle fragrances still lingered
in the room. And though his attentions had soothed her, Hans
reported that she'd done no more than lie on the bed and sob
throughout the day. Again.

"My Estelle," said Jan. He brushed the hair from before
her face, gently removing the strands that stuck to the tracks
of her tears. This was an intimacy he'd never allowed himself
with Marja. "I will protect you," he whispered to her. His lips
were mere inches above her ear, above her delicate neck, her
increasingly pale skin.

Why do I do this? he asked himself. Hans and the others
were more than sufficient to feed upon, yet Jan came back to
this poor, frightened girl time and again. Prince Garlotte had
been less than pleased; an elaborate story of a prize vacation, an
in-house lottery, had been devised for her family. But the prince
had humored Jan. *It's a small thing,* Jan knew, *but one that Garlotte
can hold over me.*

Why do I do this?

Instead of answering the question, Jan buried his face in her
silky hair. He could smell the salt of her tears and hear, louder
than thunder, the beating of her heart.

Sunday, 1 August 1999, 1:21 AM
Pendulum Avenue
Baltimore, Maryland

Gainesmil had mentioned it so casually: "My houseguest, Ms. Ash, asked me to invite you over. She hasn't had the pleasure of meeting you."

"Victoria Ash wants to meet me?" Fin had asked.

Gainesmil had assured him that it was true, and so here Fin was at the mansion. No Kindred in the city other than Gainesmil or Prince Garlotte, Fin's sire, would dare be so ostentatious, but the architect's loyalty to the prince over the years wasn't without its perks. For once, Fin felt scruffy in his shiny leather jacket and black boots. He followed a formally attired servant into the atrium as the valet pulled away in Fin's Camaro.

"Right this way, sir." The butler or manservant or whatever the hell he was led Fin up a massive, curving staircase and along a spacious hall adorned with portraits and wall-sized mirrors. A few brass fixtures provided plenty of illumination, reflecting in the infinite regression of the mirrors. Fin was uncomfortably aware of his boots squeaking with each step along the highly polished tile floor.

Finally the man opened a door into a relatively small, intimate parlor, and there sat Victoria Ash. As the servant let himself out, she rose to greet Fin and took him by the hands. "Come. Sit with me." She led him across the room to a comfortable pair of chairs. "It's so good of you to come visit me," she said, as she settled back into her seat.

"I guess you've been pretty busy since you got into town," Fin offered. He wasn't sure exactly what to say. After all, she was the one who'd asked him to stop by. Victoria's relaxed manner was disarming, yet there was something Fin couldn't quite put his finger on, a certain tension, just from sitting this close to her. She wore a loose-fitting satin blouse, and a long skirt that lay draped along her legs down to her ankles. Her lips, Fin couldn't help notice, were full and red, the envy of any model. They reminded him a bit of Morena, but he found himself unable to bring the image of his love to mind.

"Alexander speaks fondly of you," Victoria said. It took a moment to sink in. *Alexander.* Prince Garlotte. His *sire.* "He did? Of me?" Fin found that hard to believe, and he'd never heard anyone refer to the prince as Alexander.

"He most certainly does," said Victoria, and the reassuring sincerity of her words was undeniable. "As for my being busy," she continued, "there's actually very little for me to do here. You know how men are—all wanting to protect me from the grueling and dangerous work of defending a city."

"Well, the Sabbat's nothing to mess around with," Fin said. "Have you ever—"

"So it was very thoughtful of you to come see me," Victoria cut him off and nudged the conversation in a different direction. "You know," she said, placing a finger to her inviting lips, "Alexander hasn't said as much, but I do believe that you are the one he's grooming to succeed him as prince some night."

Fin couldn't help but laugh at that. "You must have me mixed up with Isaac."

Victoria patted his knee to forestall his protest.

"No. Isaac is an able sheriff, but I think Alexander has grander designs for you."

Her words, so absurd just a moment ago, seemed to gather merit upon reflection. Fin compared Victoria's impression with his own recent determination to take a more active role in the affairs of Baltimore's Kindred population.

"I mean no slight to your blood kin," said Victoria. She reached over and brushed back a lock of Fin's hair. "But there are depths to you that I don't see in Isaac."

Fin faltered momentarily. It wasn't that he disagreed with Victoria. Quite the contrary. He just had never before heard anyone else articulate thoughts so similar to his own. "I...I've been meaning...for a while now, to take a more...to be more assertive. I've...I've tried to talk to Katrina about it..."

"Katrina. Hmph." A frown darkened Victoria's countenance. Fin suddenly wanted to massage the furrow from her brow.

"You've met Katrina."

Victoria's scowl deepened. "I have. We spoke, but the conversation was...brief. And not particularly rewarding."

"She can be like that."

"I suspect she's too absorbed with her childer." Again Fin missed a beat, then he realized what Victoria must have meant. "She stays with Jazz and Tarika, but they're not..." he shook his head, "Prince Garlotte never gave us permission to Embrace anyone."

"Oh, of course they're her childer," Victoria explained patiently. She was smiling sweetly again, and that made Fin feel better. "Alexander may not have given you permission *publicly.* You know—favoritism and all that."

Slowly it dawned on Fin that Victoria could be right. He'd kind of wondered in the past, but he'd never gone so far as to ask anyone. He'd just assumed that Katrina's companions were... well, just that—companions, not childer. Fin thought of Morena, of how his heart ached for her to join him throughout eternity, but still he couldn't manage to picture her face. There was only Victoria, sitting so near, leaning close and so concerned for him.

"Katrina," Fin said with crumbling disbelief. "*She* Embraced them. You really think so?"

"I do. I think that stubborn streak is what endears her to Alexander. He prefers assertive childer." Victoria's words flowed like honey. They lifted Fin up and helped him see the heights he could hope to achieve. "And let me tell you what else I think...."

Sunday, 1 August 1999, 10:15 PM
Hemperhill Road
Baltimore, Maryland

Jan sat patiently. There was little else he *could* do. He couldn't force Prince Vitel to speak. Many minutes had passed since Jan had asked his question, but still Vitel pondered. Still he did not answer.

A huge gold-framed mirror dominated the study. The piece covered most of an entire wall, from chair rail to ceiling, and reflected the two Kindred who sat before it. Both were attired in modem business suits—Jan's cut to the latest European fashion, befitting his more frequent contact with the mortal world; Vitel's reflecting more classic lines, timeless in style and craftsmanship.

Jan had spoken with Marcus Vitel numerous times over the past two weeks, but this was Jan's first visit to the deposed prince's "home away from home," his sanctuary in a strange city.

One sanctuary of many, I suspect, Jan thought, despite the fact that his assistants had been unable to link any property deeds to Vitel, including that of this townhouse. Kindred of Vitel's standing—he was certainly one of the most influential Ventrue on the continent, though he had seldom involved himself in matters beyond his own city—generally maintained multiple havens spread throughout a handful of cities. Baltimore being so close to Washington, Jan imagined that Vitel kept several places of refuge at the ready.

A prince faced many challenges: unruly Anarchs, vindictive childer, ambitious primogen, roving packs of Sabbat, to name a few. The wise prince was not above resorting to forced exile when circumstances dictated. For an exiled prince, there was always the chance, no matter the passing of countless years, that he would return and reclaim his city.

Such was the declared intent of Marcus Vitel.

It was a goal toward which Jan wished Vitel luck but could offer little aid or hope. The Camarilla would be lucky to hold on to Baltimore, lucky not to be muscled off the entire East Coast—much less take back Washington. But the more successful Jan was in pursuing his goals, the more likely that Vitel might some night achieve his own. The prince in exile had proven relatively helpful in the Camarilla's desperate quest to stymie the Sabbat. Vitel had not, like a certain Toreador, attempted to co-opt the defense of Baltimore as a vehicle for personal aggrandizement. He'd set in motion the wheels that had led to the curfew in Washington, and then faded into the background. *As is appropriate for a deposed prince*, Jan thought. It was the matter of the curfew specifically that brought Jan here tonight.

"There is no way," Vitel said.

The sound of the prince's voice very nearly startled Jan, so accustomed to the silence had he become. The answer was not the one Jan had been waiting for.

"There *must* be a way that the curfew can be extended beyond thirty days?" Jan prodded.

Again, Vitel did not respond at once. He was not the type to banter about ideas, to work out details by thinking aloud or in conjunction with others. He considered. He pondered. He weighed options. And when he was ready, he would speak.

His thin angular face, haggard but frozen in time before it could be aged by many wrinkles, was difficult to read. The prince's eyes, however, revealed the soul of a defeated man. Over the past weeks, Jan had observed as Vitel had withdrawn further and further from interaction with anyone. Perhaps the prince had grown increasingly aware of the stark odds against the Camarilla, against his ever returning to his city, except perhaps as a prisoner of war to be tortured by the Tzimisce fiends and then disposed of in some unthinkable way.

It was the eyes, Jan decided—the eyes along with the wisps of gray streaking Vitel's hair—that made him seem old and tired.

"There is no way," Vitel again said at last.

"The governor of Maryland is willing to keep the National Guard in the city—if the Congressional oversight committee asks." Jan passed on that news from Garlotte. "I know the troops don't do our work for us; they don't fight or hunt the Sabbat. But they do make it more difficult for the Sabbat to carry out its plans."

Vitel nodded his agreement, but not enthusiastically. "Yes. The troops and the curfew are extra obstacles for them—How can vampires get anything done when no one is supposed to be on the streets after dark?—but for the most part, order has been restored to Washington. The oversight committee will return authority to the mayor and the city council. There'd be too much public backlash otherwise. The crisis has passed. The troops will go home.

The crisis *as they see it* has passed," said Jan. "Our crisis is just beginning."

Vitel did not argue the point, and Jan knew enough to bow to the prince's superior knowledge of the inner workings of the American capital.

The two sat in silence for several minutes. Jan removed his glasses and slid them into his breast pocket. He vaguely wondered if Vitel might have any whiskey on the premises, but would have felt too foolish to ask.

Instead, Jan stared at the tiny pin that glimmered from the prince's lapel. A golden eagle. Less-informed Kindred might assume the symbol to be that of the American people, but Jan knew that Vitel's roots lay among the rubble of the Roman Empire, and that there was more conquering legionnaire than New World democrat in the prince.

Jan started to ask again, to press the point: *Are you completely sure? Don't give up on me just because you've lost your damned city. There's more at stake here!* But he knew better. Because of who his sire was, Jan was given great latitude among Kindred of the Camarilla, but he could overstep those bounds. To do so would only harm his cause. And the cause was everything. The mission assigned him by Hardestadt must come before all.

"Once martial law is no longer in effect in Washington," Jan said, falling victim to the solemnity of his host, "the Sabbat will have that much more free a hand."

Vitel nodded silently.

There will be nothing to stop them, Jan continued in his mind. *They've had time to regroup after their victories. They'll be able to bring their full strength to bear.*

Jan stood. He gazed at the prince and himself in the huge mirror. At *least we've had time to prepare as well,* he thought, but he was not much comforted.

Vitel seemed lost in his own thoughts. Jan did not disturb him, but slipped from the study and showed himself out.

Morena caught sight of something in her peripheral vision, but she still wasn't expecting a person to be there when she turned toward the window.

"Ah!"

Her scream cut the night like a gunshot. She started so severely that she almost stumbled over a chair.

"Fin! You stupid jerk! Why do you always have to do that?"

"I don't always."

"*Almost* always. Close enough..." Morena struggled for an adequate expression of her displeasure, "damn it. And stop that! Don't you dare laugh at me."

Fin gave her that innocent look that he was so good at, the one that was supposed to say either *I'm not laughing*, or *I can't help it*. Two sides of the same lie. He was still crouching in the window sill like some big, sneaky, blood-sucking monkey.

"You know what I think?" she said at last. "I think you're just too impressed with yourself. Sure you can climb up the garage, and you can move around without normal people hearing you, so you sneak up on them. Because you *can*. It's a power thing."

Fin's expression grew mockingly serious. "Does it have anything to do with the patriarchic hegemony?"

"That too. And don't think I don't know you're making fun of me."

"I think you read too much."

Morena crossed her arms, then walked over to him at the window. "You told me that somebody could shoot you and it wouldn't really hurt you, that you're practically indestructible. Was that the truth?"

"Yes." Fin cocked his head and looked at her funny.

"Good." Morena gave him a quick shove, and suddenly the window was empty. She walked back to the table and sat with a sigh.

After just a minute, Fin was in the window again. This time, he didn't try to hide his grin. "That was pretty good."

"You knew I was going to do that. Didn't you?" she almost accused him. Despite her little show of defiance, she was feeling defeated. She strongly suspected that whatever paltry amount of control she exercised in this relationship, it was only because Fin let her. Fin humored her.

"No. I didn't, actually." He climbed into her tiny garage apartment, took the other chair, and sat across the table from her.

"But even if I surprised you, you could have caught yourself, or grabbed my hands before I was able to push you. Right?"

He seemed sobered by the seriousness of her tone. "Yes," he said. "I could've done either of those, or moved out of the way before you touched me."

Morena nodded but said nothing for a long while. She felt like she was on the cusp of some new understanding. Many of the vague feelings and incompletely formed thoughts that assailed her whenever Fin was around, whenever she wondered about him and his existence, were beginning to come together in some sort of form. Like Fin crouched in her window, she was between two worlds: one brightly illuminated and familiar; the other dark and dangerous, a step into oblivion.

Fin wanted her to take that step, to leave the bright, familiar world behind and follow him to the place where he knew all, and she nothing. *Where he'd have complete control*, Morena thought.

"You need to come with me," he said.

Morena looked at him quizzically. *Can you read my thoughts too?* she wondered, but his expression was not so knowing. His words mimicked her thoughts, but he was talking about something else.

"Not...for good," he explained. "This place isn't safe. This whole area between Washington and Baltimore. I've told you about some of the others…like me."

Morena nodded. He'd mentioned that there were others, but that's all he'd ever said.

Fin seemed uncomfortable talking about…whatever he was talking about. He pressed his palms flat on the table, fidgeted in his chair, ran his fingers through his dark hair, put his hands on the table again. "There's a war among my kind. It might come through here. Probably will come right through here."

"And I need to go with you," Morena said. "What about my parents?"

"I can try to work out a place for them too. It doesn't have to be for good, or that far away. Although a vacation might be a good idea. Where have you and your parents always wanted to go? I can get the money." He paused, then managed a nervous smile. "I'll even take care of your gerbils."

For a moment, Morena was ready to agree. He seemed different tonight. She wasn't sure exactly how. She felt that maybe this time he was sincere about what he thought was best for her, not necessarily just what he wanted. But she couldn't trust her feelings. Was what she felt for him *real*, or was it part of some hold he had over her? She could never be sure.

"I'm not going anywhere."

Her words sparked hours of debate, argument, tears and accusations. But Morena was decided.

Saturday, 7 August 1999, 12:25 AM
McHenry Auditorium, Lord Baltimore Inn
Baltimore, Maryland

"And yes, Prince Vitel, the attacks along the Fort Meade line—they don't really rise to the level of *attacks*—those raids have been the only direct challenge to our defenses. But of course, the state of emergency in Washington—the curfew, the National Guard troops—that's over now." Isaac's briefing of the assembled Kindred was concise and informative. He showed no signs of being intimidated by speaking before two princes and an equal number of Camarilla officials, if Jan was considered such. His role was considerably less formal than that of Archon Theo Bell.

Isaac had shown some skill for organization, as had Robert Gainesmil, and the two were intimately familiar with Baltimore and the surrounding areas, but it was Jan's hand that had guided the defensive strategy. He had subtly led the sheriff and the Toreador where he wanted them to go, and they had responded ably.

Since none of the information Isaac conveyed was new to Jan, the Dutchman withdrew somewhat from the discussion. He listened less to the actual words of the twelve Kindred present, and more to the tenor in which they were spoken. Like a lens changing focus from the detailed foreground to the broader landscape, Jan opened himself to broad impressions, most notable of which was the cathedral-like imbalance between the surrounding space of the auditorium and the number of persons in it. Instead of the riotous mob from the earlier conferences, there were only a dozen individuals present. They sat in office chairs around a stolid, square table, its corners themselves squared so that four equidistant places of honor existed. The five rows of amphitheater seats were empty. The sight of the vacant chairs prompted Jan to glance toward Victoria who, as if on cue, broke in on Isaac's current explanation of force deployments.

"First of all," she said, "I must take exception to the term *refugee*. It suggests unwashed Africans or Kosovars and simply is not acceptable. Now, you said that the majority of the displaced Kindred, among whom I count myself, thank you, have been placed along the third and fourth perimeters, those closest to the edge of the city itself."

"That's correct." Isaac was prepared to clarify any detail for her. "Many of the...uh...guests to our city are not necessarily militarily inclined, so we've stationed them on the final lines of defenses. By the time it would be necessary for them to face Sabbat attackers, it would mean that the forces from the first two lines—the Brujah, along with the prince's...Prince Garlotte's, that is, security force, and the elements from Chicago—would have fallen back, so the line would be strong enough—"

"That's very nice," Victoria interrupted him. "Is it safe to say, then, that if these guests, as you put it, were needed, there would be some notice?"

Isaac didn't answer right away.

"We would have warning?" she prompted him. "There would be a major attack. They would likely have several hours to take up their positions."

Isaac nodded slowly. "That seems likely. Yes."

"Then why is it necessary for them to be in position tonight?"

Again, Isaac paused. Jan could see that the sheriff didn't realize where Victoria was going with her question, though it should have been painfully obvious.

"Why," Victoria pressed, "are they being denied the chance to have a voice in their own destiny?"

"An attack could come at any time," Isaac tried to explain. "The Sabbat forces—"

"But you yourself just said that there would be several hours to prepare before any attack could reach the inner lines."

"It would be possible to take up the defensive positions on

short notice," Isaac conceded, "but that doesn't mean we want—"

Victoria slammed her fist on the table. "This is a deliberate attempt to manipulate these Kindred. There is no sound military reason—"

"Ms. Ash." Jan had been about to come to young Isaac's aid but, from the first of the four seats of honor, the sheriff's sire spoke a moment sooner. Without raising his voice, his words abbreviated Victoria's gathering rant. The auditorium suddenly seemed immensely large and silent.

Prince Garlotte spoke calm, joyless words. "My military planners," he gestured to the individuals around the table, "the sheriff, Mr. Gainesmil, Mr. Bell, Mr. Pieterzoon—have made what arrangements they deemed necessary."

Gainesmil, at Garlotte's left hand, shifted uncomfortably in his seat. Jan suspected that the architect was having second thoughts about information he'd passed along to his Toreador houseguest, information that might now cause a public confrontation with his prince.

"No guest in my city," said Garlotte, "is compelled to stay."

Victoria stiffened slightly. Though the prince spoke to the emptiness of the auditorium and, ostensibly, regarding the refugees manning the defenses, the implication of his statement for her was clear.

"As for the matter of various Kindred determining their own destiny," continued the prince, "customs may have differed with Prince Benison in Atlanta before the attack, but in Baltimore, the prince consults with his council of primogen as he sees appropriate. Considering the unusual circumstances at present, this body," he opened his hands to indicate all those around the table, "is serving in an advisory capacity as an ad hoc council of primogen. Should we choose to function by plebiscite, we become no better than the Sabbat, our enemies, who follow the loudest voice and the sharpest sword." Garlotte, elbows on the table before him, clasped his hands together and then rested his lips upon his knuckles. "Would you not agree, Mr. Gainesmil?" The prince's words, though his mouth was obstructed, seemed to echo throughout the chamber. He did not turn to face his lieutenant. There was no need.

Gainesmil's face, already pale, blanched. "Certainly, my prince."

Jan repressed a smile. Gainesmil might play games with his loyalty, but should he stray too far, he'd be called to task. Jan waited for Victoria's response. The prince had scored rhetorical points, but she would still argue the specifics of the situation at hand. Or so Jan expected. Instead, Victoria remained silent. The prince was not so friendly toward her as he'd been. Her play for populist leadership was dashed, and her primary confederate was publicly cowed. Was all this enough to dissuade her from seeking further undue influence?

Doubtful, thought Jan.

Since arriving in Baltimore, he'd found her willing to play the weak gambit (and fail) rather than bide her time. There was a certain desperation about her actions—or perhaps it was merely the Toreador penchant for shortsightedness and instant gratification. The clan lacked patience. They were predisposed toward rashness, unlike the Ventrue, who thrived with methodical and measured plans.

Victoria did not remain silent—that would have been too much to hope for—but much to Jan's surprise, she struck more of a conciliatory pose:

"I concede, of course, to your wishes, Prince Garlotte. Though I might suggest that the extraordinary circumstances call more for a conclave than a council of primogen, you have decided otherwise." She bowed her head respectfully.

"Well then," said Jan, hoping to move the discussion along. He was seated directly across from Prince Garlotte, in another of the four places of honor. Prince Vitel of Washington and Theo Bell occupied the other two "corner" seats, figuratively above Jan but beneath Garlotte. "Theo, your raids, have continued to—"

"Before we hear from the esteemed archon," said Garlotte, unexpectedly interrupting Jan, "I must make one comment. Mr. Pieterzoon, make no mistake of my appreciation of the gentlemen from Chicago who are contributing to the defense of this city. My undying gratitude goes out to the several clans represented among them. However," the prince, until now still staring into the emptiness of the auditorium, fixed his gaze upon Jan, "it has come to my attention that some of them are not limiting themselves to the hunting grounds I have set aside for them."

Jan, caught off guard by this rebuke, began to respond, but even his most deferential assurances were preempted by the steel glare of the prince.

"If we hold off the enemy hordes," said Garlotte, "only to succumb to internal chaos, then the Sabbat will have triumphed."

Jan respectfully waited several moments until there was no doubt that Prince Garlotte had had his say. "I will see to it, my prince."

Behind the mollifying words, Jan's mind was racing. He had arranged the presence of the defenders from Chicago, nearly fifty of them, but he didn't command them, per se. Garlotte, however, had seen fit to chastise Jan—publicly, no less. The expression of displeasure was more significant than the specific nature of the rebuke: It was a sign to all present that this Ventrue from Europe did not run the city, had not received carte blanche from the prince.

Another aspect of Garlotte's words disturbed Jan. The prince complained of the Chicagoans ignoring hunting restrictions. Surely he knew of Jan's transgression as well. *Estelle.* The initial feeding had qualified as an emergency, but in keeping the girl after the crisis had passed, instead of clouding her memory and releasing her, Jan had blatantly ignored Garlotte's proscription. Did the prince's rebuke contain a private as well as public warning?

Jan ticked off the score in his mind: *Victoria, Gainesmil, me.* With just a few sentences, Prince Garlotte had put each in his or her place. Though Jan was not above a bit of public humility, if it made the prince feel better, the implication that Garlotte, on some level, equated Jan with the two Toreador, that the prince considered Jan a threat, was a danger sign. *Does he think I want his blasted city?* Jan wondered. *Perhaps the added security was a mistake. He could believe that I staged the assassination attempt as an excuse to strengthen my own hand.*

Jan mulled over the seemingly unending string of

possibilities as Theo described in sparse detail his latest raids around Washington. He was no longer probing far into the city; the Sabbat had grown too numerous and better organized. Jan thought at first that the Brujah seemed more relaxed than usual as he spoke, but then the chastened Ventrue corrected himself. Bell seemed exactly as he always seemed—grim, inscrutable—but he'd removed his cap and sunglasses. Probably that was as close to affable as he ever came. Bell's companion Lydia, whom he sometimes left in charge when he was away from the city, was surprisingly attentive and well-behaved for a Brujah.

Again, Jan let himself grow slightly detached from the discussion at hand. He concentrated instead on what could be gleaned from the questions asked from different quarters. Marcus Vitel continued to ask insightful questions of Bell and Isaac regarding Baltimore's defenses and Sabbat tactics. The Washington prince along with Victoria, who still questioned the others freely, were obviously the hawks among the crowd. Vitel ventured as far as to ask about a potential timetable for retaking Washington, and when assured that such a venture was patently impracticable, he grew sullen and silent.

The victims are always the most anxious to strike back, Jan thought. Vitel had lost his city. Victoria had suffered—exactly how, Jan wasn't sure—at the hands of the Sabbat. Then Jan's thoughts shifted suddenly to other victims. Would Marja and Roel have struck back? Would Estelle, cowering upstairs even as he met with his fellow undead, strike back if she could? *Or do I so completely destroy their will that they cannot?*

Jan squeezed his eyes shut until he had pushed those thoughts far back in his mind. This was not the time—if there ever were a time. The discussion continued around him. When he opened his eyes, no one seemed to have noticed his lapse, except perhaps Roughneck who was staring at him. But the Malkavian, as was his friend the Quaker, was prone to fits of staring for no reason. Jan also thought, for a moment, that Colchester was watching him, but whenever Jan glanced his way, the Nosferatu seemed intent on what Bell or Isaac or Vitel was saying.

If that really is Colchester, Jan thought. The Nosferatu wore an image that was disturbingly …normal. It was not impossible—in fact, it was common—for a Nosferatu to be seen as other than he truly was. But this mild-mannered, well-kempt black man in a business suit was nothing like the obscene, shaggy monstrosity with whom Jan had dealings. At the outset of the meeting, Colchester had apologized for his absence from the earlier conferences—he disliked crowds, he'd said—though Jan knew the Nosferatu had been present.

The business of the council meeting—the term *conference* was no longer in vogue, now that the masses were, thankfully, excluded—was continuing when the double doors at the rear of the auditorium slammed open. Malachi, the Gangrel scourge and also the only one of the twelve Kindred present who was not seated at the table, was alert at his position guarding the door. His every muscle tensed, as if he were coiled to spring, but then a shock of recognition swept over his face. Suddenly Malachi dropped to one knee and lowered his head.

Into the room, past the kneeling sentry, strode an imposing figure—taller than any in the room save possibly Bell, red hair receded but hanging far down his back, muscled legs in black leather extending from a gray cloak held together at the chest by long, distinctly claw-like fingers. Most striking was the scowl of barely restrained fury that twisted the newcomer's face. Jan had met Xaviar just three weeks ago, when the Gangrel justicar had agreed to gather a small army of his clansmen and guard Buffalo and upstate New York from Sabbat depredations.

The justicar was met with silence as he stalked down the aisle to the conference table. The impression of Xaviar's agitation grew more palpable with each step.

Queasiness took hold in Jan's gut. *They've taken Buffalo,* he thought. *The Sabbat has taken Buffalo.* If that outlying point no longer remained in Camarilla hands, then the noose was tightened around all their necks.

"Justicar Xaviar," said Prince Garlotte, when the Gangrel was sufficiently near, "how may we be of service?" The prince, despite the unannounced arrival of a justicar in his city, appeared totally composed.

With Xaviar's final few steps, the two Malkavians seated to

Jan's right abandoned their places and prudently created some distance between themselves and the justicar. Xaviar stood alone by that side of the table, scant feet from Jan on one side, Theo Bell on the other. The Gangrel took a moment to observe the other Kindred present. He seemed to calm somewhat, but the tension in his right hand, still clutching shut the cloak draped over his shoulders, was visible enough.

"We must abandon the city," Xaviar said without preamble. His words swept across the table like the first gusts of a stormwind, but instead of chaos, silence reigned.

"Has Buffalo fallen?" Jan asked at last, unable to wait for Garlotte to speak, as would have been proper, and at any rate, Garlotte would not have asked that most important question. He refused to see the strategic importance of *that other city*, as he called it, and that if the scattered Sabbat forces in the Northeast were able to join those in Washington to form a deadly ring around Baltimore, all would be lost.

Garlotte suddenly seemed less important as Jan realized Xaviar was staring down at him as if the question made no sense whatsoever.

"Buffalo," Jan tried again. "Has the Sabbat taken it?"

Xaviar allowed himself a mirthless laugh. "The Sabbat is nothing." His gaze shifted from Jan to Theo and finally to Prince Garlotte. "We must abandon the city. Every Kindred is needed."

Those around the table regarded him with varying degrees of befuddlement, curiosity, and fear. Jan believed that he saw something of madness in the Gangrel's eyes.

The Sabbat is nothing.

"I'm afraid we don't understand, Justicar," said Garlotte. "Needed for what?" The prince couldn't have been happy with the suggestion that his city be abandoned, but he trod lightly with the justicar.

Xaviar had little patience even for Garlotte. The Gangrel began to snarl, Jan thought, but then it seemed merely that a muscle at the corner of Xaviar's lip was twitching.

"The Final Nights are at hand," the Gangrel said.

The stark note of prophecy jarred Jan. The words, painted with the mingled accents from hundreds of years in the Old

Country, from the lips of the justicar touched a place within Jan as deep as his need for victims, a place as central as the hunger to what he had become. The Beast stirred within him.

The Final Nights are at hand.

Such words were sometimes uttered casually among the ignorant, or disingenuously by those hoping to strike terror into the hearts of listeners, but Xaviar was neither fool nor demagogue. He was one of seven justicars, chosen of the Camarilla to oversee its mandates. He was Gangrel, of all the clans closest to the Beast and sensitive to its emanations.

Other words of prophecy, newer words, sprang unbidden to Jan's mind:

The Gangrel was consumed by the Beast. Flesh of his flesh. Soul of his soul. And at the Tower of the Saint atop the Isle of Angels, the Unholy Triad was complete. Kinslayer. Betrayer. Beast. The Beast walks the earth. The Undoing of the Children of Caine is at hand.

The words were attributed to the Cult of the Wanderer, an obscure group of lunatics that had arisen from the ashes of the Blood Curse. The words spoke of the end of time. They spoke of Gehenna.

"What are you saying?" Garlotte tersely asked the justicar, latest in a string of Kindred telling the prince what to do with his city.

Xaviar, if possible, was even less used to and more irritated by opposition than the prince. This time, the Gangrel did snarl. "The Final Nights are at hand," he said again, as if that should explain it all, but he found himself still facing uncomprehending stares. "The prophecies are coming true!" he barked finally. "An elder power has risen. We must destroy it or be doomed!"

Jan battled mounting cognitive dissonance. His frame of reference had little room for elder powers, for the Final Nights. Futilely, he tried to reconcile the world he knew—Kindred politics, the Sabbat, princes and clans—with childish superstitions suddenly lent credence by the passion of a justicar. Not just passion, Jan realized. *Fear.*

"Elder power?" Prince Garlotte was standing now, his patience stretched to the breaking point. He waved his hand dismissively. "If some decrepit Gangrel has gotten loose in the woods—"

"No Gangrel did this!" roared Xaviar, and he pulled back his cloak and thrust forward an impossibly mangled arm. His left forearm was not broken but *twisted*, warped into unnatural curves and bends. Familiar claw-like fingers dangled from the end of the useless limb.

Jan had been edging his chair away from the Gangrel. The tension between prince and justicar had rocketed out of control, and Jan had feared violence.

Between battling elders was not the place to be. But now, with the shock of Xaviar brandishing his crippled arm, the crisis was at least temporarily averted. Garlotte, and the others, gawked openly at Xaviar's disfigurement. Victoria looked away. One of the Malkavians, the Quaker, had dropped beneath the table and was whimpering.

Theo Bell was the first to recover. "What happened?"

Xaviar's eyes were downcast now. He stared at the center of the table. "It destroyed all those I took into battle. One other escaped, maybe two…I don't know."

"How many Gangrel?" Bell asked. His deep baritone seemed to hold the terror at bay for all the Kindred.

"All those who defended Buffalo."

Bell nodded grimly.

Jan tried in vain to fathom what sort of creature could destroy such a collection of Gangrel.

"An Antediluvian," said Xaviar.

"Antedi…" Victoria gasped. The name from legend seemed to catch in her throat. She clasped a hand over her mouth and started shaking her head.

"The third generation is rising," Xaviar said. "The Dark Father will not be far behind."

Victoria's hand slid down to clutch her neck, as if her throat had been slit. "There's no such…" she whispered more to herself than to anyone else, but the proper words eluded her. "No such…"

But Xaviar heard her, and her doubt enraged him. "It called fire from the earth's belly against us! The very ground beneath our feet obeyed it!" His eyes bulged. He bared his fangs and raised his deformed arm. "It melted flesh and bone with its hands! And its eye...throbbing, pulsing." He held his right hand open as if cupping a giant orb. "To look into it, into that eye..." Xaviar's mouth twitched again; he tried to repress a shudder, "was to stare at Final Death."

Yet you escaped, Jan wanted to say—but to do so would have been to invite dismemberment, for even a one-armed Gangrel justicar was not to be trifled with.

In hurried phrases, Xaviar described the scene of carnage he'd beheld in the Adirondack foothills, far east of Buffalo— fountains of lava and fire, spikes rising from the earth to impale, slabs of stone crushing Gangrel, lakes of blood and fire. But always he came back to the eye—glowing, throbbing, holding Cainites in thrall while the risen Antediluvian tore their bodies limb from limb.

"Xaviar," said Garlotte, having regained his calm, "surely *something* attacked your people. We do not doubt you in that. But to abandon the city...?"

"*What difference are Camarilla and Sabbat when we are all destroyed?*" Xaviar shouted. "The Sabbat will fight *with* us against an Antediluvian!"

"Treason!" Vitel was on his feet and pointing an accusatory finger at Xaviar. "The Sabbat are no better than animals! I will not submit to them!"

Xaviar stepped forward, as if he would charge *through* the table. He held a clawed hand before him. His face seemed suddenly more snout-like with his bared fangs.

Despite the danger, Jan was searching his memory for any scrap of information about the Antediluvians, but regardless of the legends or prophecies recalled, he knew what his sire would say, what he *had* said, hundreds of times.

"The Antediluvians do not exist," said Jan. "We know that to be the truth, and the Sabbat, whatever propaganda its leaders may spew to control the rabble, knows it as well."

The words struck Xaviar like a blow to the face. He jerked his head around to face Jan and moved dangerously close. "*We know that to be the truth?*" he bellowed, mocking Jan. "This," he stuck his twisted arm in Jan's face, "*this* is the truth! I have seen the truth! I have stood before that eye and *felt* the truth as it toyed with my body as if I were made of soft wax!"

Xaviar turned from Jan and began pacing back and forth, waving his good hand in rage and disbelief. "We exist, no matter what the mortals think. Do the Antediluvians need our belief? Or would they rather catch us unawares?"

"Legends," said Jan. "Folk tales, myths. Nothing more." Hardestadt had always been emphatic on this point, and Jan was nothing if not well-schooled and obedient. "There must be some other explanation.

"Bah!" Xaviar flung his head so violently that he sprayed droplets of froth from the corners of his mouth. "The Ventrue can rot!" He shot a challenging glare at Prince Garlotte, but the prince folded his arms and kept his peace.

"Theo," said Xaviar, "bring your Brujah. I will gather more Gangrel. We will get Tremere sorcerers from the chantry in New York. We don't need the rest—weaklings and cowards!"

All eyes turned toward the Brujah archon. He sat perfectly still, as always keeping only his own counsel. "My instructions from Justicar Pascek are to do what I can to stop the Sabbat."

"Do you doubt what I say?" asked Xaviar, the question half entreaty, half threat.

"No." Theo didn't hesitate this time. "But Pascek would be pretty pissed off if I just dropped what I was doing, just like you'd be if one of *your* archons ignored you, and just like Hardestadt would be if Pieterzoon here up and left. Shit, Hardestadt probably has more clout than my boss and you put together."

Through narrowed eyes, Xaviar looked from face to face around the table. Only the four Kindred at the places of honor met his gaze unflinchingly: Garlotte, Theo, Vitel, Jan. Isaac and Gainesmil cast nervous glances at their prince and were careful to avoid eye contact with Xaviar. Lydia, the Brujah, did likewise except for watching Theo for nonexistent signs of his reaction. Colchester was doing what Nosferatu did best—not drawing attention to himself—while Roughneck and the Quaker were, respectively, stalking around the room mumbling, and under the table. Victoria, since the first mention of an Antediluvian, had retreated within herself. She was absorbed with her thoughts and memories, speaking to no one, perhaps not completely aware of what transpired around her.

When Xaviar turned toward Jan, the Ventrue held his gaze for quite a while. The Gangrel was a fearsome creature, but Jan had studied at the knee of a master, one of the eldest of the Camarilla. No slash of Gangrel claw could tear down the loyalty that Hardestadt had spent centuries to build—the loyalty and the fear of failure. Within Xaviar's bestial eyes, what Jan had first taken for madness now crystallized and became something else, something harder, less forgiving.

Xaviar, with great effort, took a moment to regain his composure. His good hand rubbed across the red stubble on his chin. He licked the back of his hand and, like a cat, smoothed down the hair above his left ear. All the while, the small muscle at his lip jumped, and his eyes burned with disgust. His face, still showing signs of strain, seemed more human again.

He raised his crippled arm, but this time didn't brandish it so violently. "Twelve nights ago this happened. For three nights I grieved. I roamed the mountains mad with rage. Then for six nights I hunted. I had many wounds and little strength. I hunted animals, then mortals. When I'd wandered as far west as Buffalo, I found a Sabbat pack and drank their thin blood. Then for three nights, I traveled here, all the way searching for a Gangrel seer who had spoken to my people before the massacre—it was he who told us of the Final Nights. But he was not to be found. Each of these nights, from sunset to sunrise, I fought the desire to go back to that place, to fight the creature and its eye, to die as my clansmen died. But I did not. The Camarilla must be warned, I told myself. Then together...*together*...we will go back to that place. And there will be blood and vengeance."

Again the Gangrel justicar looked from Garlotte to Bell to Vitel to Jan.

"As justicar," Xaviar said, "of Clan Gangrel, of the Camarilla, I take command of all Kindred in this city. *We will destroy the Antediluvian.*"

The shocked silence was broken only by the panicked muttering of the Quaker under the table: "Sweet Jesus...sweet Jesus..."

Then slowly, deliberately, Prince Garlotte rose to his feet. "With all due and proper respect, justicar," he said, the weight of his decision evident in each syllable, "retaining this city is the most vital interest of the Camarilla at present. We do not question your authority. Considering the dire consequences of your demand, for *all* Kindred, however, we demand a conclave."

Jan watched Xaviar closely. Though the Gangrel had seemed close to violence with both princes earlier, this gambit by Garlotte, no matter what he said, and though technically sound, was a tremendous affront to the justicar. Xaviar, on edge as he was, might snap. Politics be damned. The only question then would be who would support Garlotte to Final Death. And who would stand by and watch.

Xaviar flexed the claws of his right hand, stretching the long digits and curling them in, over and over, without seeming to realize he was doing so. His gaze bore into Garlotte. "Who will stand against me?" he growled at last. "Let there be no confusion."

A long silence passed, finally broken by Jan: "The Antediluvians do not exist." His lot was thrown in with Garlotte, though, considering the unyielding position of Jan's sire, he had little real choice.

"So speaks the slave of Hardestadt." Xaviar turned to Theo.

Bell slowly shook his head. "I have a job to do here. Until we know more…"

"So speaks the slave of Pascek."

"Aid us against the Sabbat," said Prince Garlotte, trying to offer the justicar a way out of this confrontation without losing face, "then we will see to this…this other matter."

"So speaks the slave to his city," Xaviar said, turning from prince to deposed prince. "Vitel?"

"There are other dangers in the world," Marcus Vitel said, "but I will have my city back, and I will see the Sabbat destroyed. Or myself in the attempt." Jan sat perfectly still. Though the threat of violence had passed, something more monumental now hung in the balance. It was clear that Xaviar could not hope to prevail through a conclave. His response might well change the course of Kindred history.

A soul-baring growl began deep in the justicar's throat, only barely taking the form of words by the time it escaped his mouth. "Then damn you all, slaves of the Antediluvians." He took a long time and regarded each Kindred in turn, as if branding their visage in his memory. "Damn you all. For this I swear: I will see that creature dead, and its eye ground to dust. And if first I have to drink an ocean of blood to be again whole of body, it will be the blood of your clansmen." He thrust a finger toward Garlotte. "And yours," toward Bell.

Then he turned to Jan. "And perhaps the blood of your sire."

Despite Jan's best efforts, the threat struck rage into his heart, not from fear that Xaviar would carry it out, but from the lack of respect conveyed for Hardestadt. Jan rose partially from his seat. Only a supreme effort of will kept him from launching a fist at the Gangrel's jaw—a suicidal prospect, and no doubt what Xaviar was hoping for.

Jan lowered himself back into the chair. "I assure you, honorable justicar, it is not lightly nor with any pleasure that we refuse your request."

Xaviar sneered. With his good hand he leaned forward onto the table. "Save your words for those who would listen." He glanced meaningfully at Theo. "Though I would have expected better of the Brujah than to sell themselves cheaply to Ventrue masters."

Bell responded not in the least to the justicar's baiting.

"Very well, then." Xaviar dug his claws into the table top. "The Final Nights are at hand. I leave the blind to lead the blind. This is not the first time the clans of the Camarilla have shown their disdain for the sacrifices of the Gangrel. But it will be the last." With a quick raking motion, he gouged out a handful of wood and ground it to splinters in his hand. Then slowly, he let the remnants sift through his fingers. "See how well you find your way without us. Tell your masters if you wish. I'll tell them soon enough in person. Let the union be dissolved."

As Xaviar stalked from the silent chamber, Jan didn't fully notice Victoria still trapped within her own mind, a finger absently stroking the near-perfect jaw. He didn't see the ebon statue that was Theo Bell, nor the Malkavian hugging his shoulders in a far corner, nor the other madman curled into fetal position on the floor, nor the others staring dumbstruck after the justicar.

Instead, Jan saw the portico of an ancient temple, a temple that was the only hope of civilization—seven mammoth columns supporting the structure that protected learning and law and order. Only now, one of the seven pillars had cracked and toppled to the ground, where it lay smashed beyond repair. And Jan had pushed it.

part three:

progeny

A solemn collection of Kindred had gathered around the scarred conference table. Jan, like each of the others, did his best not to look at the gouged crater in the wood just a few feet away, but he found his gaze drawn back to the spot time and again.

"Surely the entire clan won't leave the Camarilla," said Gainesmil, "no matter what Xaviar says."

Jan followed the Toreador's nervous glance at the rear of the auditorium, where Malachi stood guard by the doors that, mere hours ago, Xaviar had stormed through. Garlotte's scourge had not left with the justicar—not yet—but most Gangrel, unlike Malachi, were not tied so closely to a particular prince or to Camarilla hierarchy.

"If anyone speaks for all the Gangrel," said Jan morosely, his eyes now locked on the evidence of violence done the table, "it is Xaviar. Word will spread. There will be a mass exodus."

"Word has *already* spread," Prince Garlotte snapped.

They had all agreed last night to keep Xaviar's outburst and threats secret for as long as possible. To Garlotte's disgust, that had proven to be only a few hours. He glared around the table.

Their number was fewer tonight. Isaac and Lydia were overseeing portions of the defenses. The Quaker apparently had been so shocked by Xaviar's pronouncements of doom that the Malkavian had fallen into torpor, and Colchester was nowhere to be seen.

Not to say that he's not here, Jan mused morbidly. The weight of responsibility he'd felt for so many weeks had been replaced—or maybe added to—by numbing fatalism. The Gangrel would leave. The Camarilla cities would fall one by one. Jan would fail his mission and, if he survived, return to face Hardestadt.

"What about Buffalo?" Theo Bell asked.

What about Buffalo? thought Jan. *It will fall. Without the Gangrel, it will fall.* He almost spoke the words aloud—more prophecies of doom; *the Undoing of the Children of Caine is at hand*—but he restrained himself. Bell's focus on details, his enduring pragmatism and unbreakable will, drew Jan back to a challenge that was not yet completely hopeless. Not yet. He straightened somewhat in his chair as his thoughts turned in a more productive direction. He could not afford to escape through madness and torpor, as the Quaker had. Nor could Jan retreat inward, like Victoria. She sat at the table again tonight, a pained expression on her face, only speaking when directly addressed. She was not herself. Xaviar's doom-mongering had affected her perhaps even more deeply than it had the unstable Quaker.

But more important matters required Jan's attention.

"Buffalo is completely exposed without the Gangrel," he said. "If we shift forces from here...maybe the Chicago element—"

"I cannot accept the weakening of this city," Garlotte broke in. His words were sharp, unequivocal.

Jan tried to explain, "If we create a small, mobile force, then it could be brought back if—"

"Baltimore must be held," Garlotte insisted. "If we divide our forces, neither city will be strong enough to stand."

"I agree," Marcus Vitel added. "We stay strong here and press the war south when we are able."

Jan recognized from Garlotte's tone that the prince would not negotiate on this point, and though Jan had been allowed great leeway in coordinating the Camarilla defenses, he was still, in the end, a guest in Garlotte's city. Additionally, with *both* princes agreeing and Theo not feeling compelled to offer his opinion, Jan held little hope of swaying those to whom, technically, he was merely an advisor.

"Abandon Buffalo," Gainesmil said.

"No." Jan removed his glasses and began to rub the bridge of his nose. Despite the hopelessness of his position, he felt compelled to make them see the importance of somehow maintaining Buffalo. "Baltimore is stronger," he explained, "if there is the threat of another Camarilla city within striking distance should the Sabbat fall on us here...or if there's at least a *perceived* threat."

Garlotte regarded him skeptically but said nothing.

Jan opened his mouth to speak, but, surprisingly, it was Bell who gave voice to his plan: "As long as the Sabbat *think* there's an army that can come help us here, that's as good as having an army. We bluff them."

"Yes," Jan agreed.

Garlotte was shaking his head. "But they *will* find out about the Gangrel, and if we don't divert forces from here, how do we make them think—"

"We make an army," said Jan. He set his glasses on the table, then stood and began to pace back and forth behind the empty seats, where Xaviar had stood the night before. *Damn his pride*, Jan thought, seeing again the Gangrel's mark on the table. *And damn Garlotte's. And damn mine.* But there had been no other way than to defy the justicar.

Now it was Vitel shaking his head. "You're not suggesting that we just Embrace enough mortals to defend a city."

Jan paused in his pacing. "That's exactly what I'm suggesting. Theo—what?" Jan could tell the archon didn't like the idea.

The Brujah's dark face was creased by a deep frown. "I don't think Pascek would go for it."

"Would he rather lose the entire East Coast?"

"Maybe," Bell said. "All I know is he and some of the other bigwigs have had a hundred shit fits over Prince Michaela Embracing an army in New York. It's not the Embracing exactly, but that's a lot of tough Ventrue bastards. No offense."

But Jan wasn't prepared to concede. "What good is a balance of power among our own clans if the Sabbat takes everything?"

Bell shrugged. "Don't ask me. Ask Pascek. Ask Hardestadt."

Jan understood Theo's point readily enough. His sire would

not approve of the plan. Bell was right. More than the East Coast was at stake. What good would be saving the East Coast if in doing so they brought the Camarilla clans to each other's throats? Already, the Gangrel had abandoned the sect. No one would agree to an army of Ventrue or—God forbid—Tremere, for the very reason that those clans were already seen by each other as being too powerful. But that still left other options.

Jan turned to face Bell. "What about a small army of Nosferatu…and some Brujah tossed in?"

"They'd be so young," said Vitel. "Even if they were of potent blood, it takes time to adjust to our existence, to master the gifts of the undead."

"But it's a bluff." Bell slowly began to nod. "They don't have to master anything."

"Exactly," said Jan. "They don't have to fend off an attack. If there's enough Kindred activity, it could confuse Sabbat spies and delay an attack. It'll at least buy us time, and with Buffalo in Camarilla hands, Baltimore is stronger." Jan closed his hand into a fist. He unobtrusively glanced at Garlotte, who seemed less entrenched in his opposition. *He'll agree as long as we don't take anything from here*, Jan thought.

Vitel, however, was not convinced. "The clans might not mind all those new Cainites, but Prince Lladislas in Buffalo won't like it. Overpopulating doesn't make for stability."

"Neither does a horde of Sabbat running through the street killing mortals and staking the prince," Bell pointed out. He shrugged. "But he's right. Lladislas won't like it."

Jan returned to his seat. "It's the best chance he has to keep his city." But he knew they were correct. Lladislas was a hardheaded Brujah—as if *any* prince wasn't stubborn—and he'd spend years arguing for reinforcements rather than accept a plan that might leave him stuck with a gaggle of ill-disciplined, hunger-driven neonates to wreck the Masquerade in Buffalo.

"What if we tell him that our intelligence shows that an attack is imminent?" Jan suggested. "We tell him an attack is coming. We can't reinforce him—which is true. This way, he can at least leave an army of neonates to take a few Sabbat with them. No recriminations from the Camarilla."

"He'd like that," Bell agreed.

"Lladislas evacuates the city," Jan continued. "With the increased Kindred activity, the Sabbat believes there's a real, formidable army. They're deterred from attacking...*or* if they send a force large enough to deal with what they think is there, they'll have to draw manpower from Washington, and we have a chance to strike there."

This last line of reasoning broke through to Vitel. He agreed with anything that would give the Camarilla a chance to win back his city. Garlotte, too, was willing to go along—which meant Gainesmil was on board—since Baltimore was not weakened. Roughneck didn't pull much weight even if he did object for some reason. Practically speaking, there was still one potential veto.

"Lladislas will do it... if you tell him to," Jan said to Theo. It was a tricky thing, to ask a Brujah archon to mislead a Brujah prince, and Jan couldn't press too hard. It was a call Theo had to make. Jan only hoped the archon realized that there truly were no ulterior motives for trying to get the Brujah prince out of his city. "It's in his best interest, and he won't go along otherwise."

Theo sat stone-faced. He had contributed to the plan, but much of the execution would necessarily fall on his shoulders. Finally, Bell nodded, if not enthusiastically. "It's his best shot," he agreed, "and it's the Camarilla's best shot."

"We might as well be the Sabbat."

All heads turned to face Victoria, who had unexpectedly offered her first opinion of the evening.

"We might as well be the Sabbat," she said again in a low voice. Her green eyes seemed to have lost their luster. Though she never looked poorly enough to be thought of as haggard, she did seem tired, and only vaguely concerned with events around her.

Jan didn't completely follow her meaning. He didn't think she could change the minds of the others, but she did exhibit influence with Prince Garlotte on occasion, so Jan attempted to mollify her. "We have to convince Prince Lladislas to act in his own best interest, otherwise—"

"Lie to the damned Brujah all you want!" she suddenly

blurted out. "We all do. They never know the difference."

If Bell took offense behind his unreadable mask, he gave no sign.

"But to Embrace twenty...fifty, a hundred mortals?" she went on. "To turn them loose on the streets? That does nothing for the Masquerade—nothing good. It makes us no better than the Sabbat. Is it worth surviving, only to become what we despise?"

"If it's the only way we *can* survive," Jan retorted. He was somewhat mystified by Victoria's sudden bout of scruples. Law, morality—these were not absolutes, as she seemed suddenly to think. Like manners, they were preferences contrived to govern the interaction of the masses. But sometimes those individuals occupying positions of responsibility, those Kindred entrusted with the caretaking of the entire race—of humanity, fragile as it was—must through necessity step beyond those bounds.

Jan started to say as much, but the attention of all around the table was distracted by movement at the rear of the auditorium. Malachi had stepped closer to the double doors and was prepared for whomever entered. Jan had visions of Xaviar again slamming open the doors and stalking down the aisle, but Malachi hadn't heard the Gangrel justicar approach until the doors were flung open wide.

When the doors did open, Prince Garlotte's youngest childe, Fin, entered the auditorium. He seemed embarrassed for a moment that everyone was watching him, but he quickly mastered himself and continued down to the table.

"Our business here is concluded," said Prince Garlotte. "Mr. Pieterzoon, Mr. Bell, proceed with your plan." Then, having dismissed Victoria's objection, he directed his attention toward Fin.

For his part, the young Ventrue, aside from a brief glance at Victoria, who didn't seem to notice he was there, determinedly held his sire's gaze. "Prince Garlotte," he said formally, "I must discuss something with you, and since it's something you have to decide as prince, and not just as my sire, I come to you here."

"I can see that you do," Garlotte said evenly.

Fin paused and licked his lips. Jan found himself sympathetic to the boy's plight of addressing an aloof, seemingly omnipotent sire. Though the council proper was concluded, the other Kindred remained at their seats out of respect for Garlotte and his childe. Fin seemed to have expected more resistance from his sire. Encountering none, he plowed ahead.

"I want to Embrace a mortal. I've never asked for this before." He hesitated briefly, then, "I feel that it's my right."

"Your right." Prince Garlotte did not laugh or grow angry. He remained totally impassive.

"Yes. Katrina has Embraced. Twice. I don't think it's too much to ask."

Jan couldn't help but take note of the boy's resolve—and of his utter lack of judgment. Apparently every Kindred in Baltimore knew about the prince's troublesome female childe and her unauthorized coterie, but to bring to the prince's attention facts that he obviously wanted *not* to know—at least officially—was less than wise.

"You are aware of all that is transpiring?" Prince Garlotte asked. "All that consumes my time—the Sabbat hordes pressing at the city gate; the insanity of a justicar? Surely you've heard of these."

"I am." Fin swallowed hard. He paused, but then pressed ahead. "I want to Embrace Morena before something happens. With the Sabbat. Before it's too late."

Garlotte rested his chin on his fist. The assembly, quite ill at ease now, waited patiently nonetheless for him to resolve the matter. "Come to me, my childe."

Several seconds passed before Fin took the first step. Each footfall echoed through the otherwise silent auditorium as he walked around the table. Fin knelt before his sire, the prince, and bowed his head.

Garlotte lifted his childe's chin. "You must learn patience. A year and a night—before that time is up, we will resolve this. Speak no more of it to me."

Fin nodded and rose. A mix of relief and disappointment was visible on his face, but Jan couldn't help thinking that the young Ventrue was fortunate.

Sunday, 8 August 1999, 1:42 AM
Presidential Suite, Lord Baltimore Inn
Baltimore, Maryland

"You're sure there's no indication of an attack on Buffalo?" Jan asked.

Colchester had waited until van Pel left to reveal himself. He wore his monstrous, tusked visage and resembled nothing of the suave businessman who last night had sat at council. "No large-scale movements from Washington, or from Montreal or New York City," he said. "And Vykos's ghoul reports only the continued build-up for an eventual shot at Baltimore."

"The Assamite masquerading as Vykos's ghoul."

"Yes. Parmenides, now Ravenna."

"And this other business with the Assamites…"

"Right." Colchester stretched and cracked his knuckles so loudly that Jan thought the Nosferatu's fingers might pop off. "Since the Sabbat War started, four Tremere assassinated: in Atlanta, right here in Baltimore, then Calcutta, then New York. All four confirmed or strongly suspected Assamite involvement. I mean, shit, who else is gonna go around bumping off warlocks?"

"But who are they working for?" Jan wondered aloud. "Assamites don't dirty their hands for free."

"They didn't used to, anyway," Colchester said. "Word is that might've changed."

Jan was only partially listening as he tried to unravel certain facts. "And Vykos has a personal Assamite. Has he…she…it, whatever…Vykos made an alliance with them?"

"Possible. There's also a Setite." Colchester started counting off on his fingers. "Operates out of Baltimore, had a flunky in Atlanta, and was in Calcutta *meeting with* that one when he got whacked. Three out of four."

"Hm." Jan weighed this information against his own suspicions. "Prince Garlotte knows this Setite?" Colchester nodded. "Sure. Hesha keeps a low profile. It's not worth starting a war to get rid of him."

"Hesha Ruhadze? I didn't know he worked out of Baltimore."

"He don't advertise."

"I see. There's also Victoria," Jan pointed out, "who was in Atlanta, and meeting with Maria Chin when she was assassinated."

"Maybe the Assamites gave out Tremere coupons…."

Jan was thinking aloud again and paying little attention to Colchester's prattle. "That might explain why Aisling Sturbridge is spending her time at the chantry in New York instead of here."

"…Maybe it was a Tremere rebate, or off one get one free. Tax write-off?"

Jan's thoughts, despite his best efforts, drifted away from murdered Tremere and back to Victoria. Part of him recoiled at the thought of her being responsible for or even complicit in such brutality. Maria Chin had been decapitated by a garrotte. Jan pictured Victoria, not as an accomplice luring the Tremere to her destruction, but as a victim, horrified, cowering in fear. That image blended with how he'd seen her tonight—practically catatonic. She seemed so fragile.

But Jan knew that wasn't the full story. Ironically enough, it was Colchester's absurd litany that helped Jan clear his mind and focus again on the business at hand.

"Never mind." Jan waved Colchester silent. "Who's behind it isn't the most important thing right now." *We can do with a few less Tremere*, he thought, but then caught himself. The Tremere could be a devastating tool when unleashed against an enemy. *But they'd damn well better start pulling their weight.*

"Now," Jan said to Colchester, "this is what we're going to do…."

Sunday, 8 August 1999, 4:19 AM
A subterranean grotto
New York City, New York

For the past forty-five minutes, Calebros had stared into the dark recesses of his lair and tried to calm himself. Still, his hands were not completely free of trembling. Upon receiving the news, he had managed to clack out the relevant data on his typewriter before succumbing to the nervous palsy. Reading the understatements recorded in ink did little to soothe him.

The solution to a puzzle that had dogged him for weeks might very well be revealing itself to him, *but at what price?*

8 August 1999
Re: Gangrel

Baltimore, Colchester reports----
Xaviar claims Gangrel to quit
Camarilla; the justicar is not given to
idle threats! Claims Antediluvian
destroyed all Gangrel, upstate NY;
referred to prophecies of Endtime,
"Final Nights at hand."

Xaviar repeatedly mentioned
Antediluvian's eye---connection to
Eye of Hazimel?

file action update: EoH

*Have Jeremiah begin
observation of Anatole.
Just in case.*

Sunday, 8 August 1999, 11:59 PM
Pendulum Avenue
Baltimore, Maryland

"Is there anything I may do for you, Ms. Ash?"

"Yes, Langford. You may go away."

Normally Gainesmil's butler would slip silently from the room, but tonight with every step he crushed fragments of glass beneath the soles of his painstakingly polished shoes. Only when she heard the door click shut did Victoria open her eyes. She couldn't face anyone. Not tonight. She couldn't stand the thought of someone looking at her. She couldn't face even her own eyes. And she wouldn't have to. Not now. Every mirror, every vase with a reflective surface, every glass face from the pictures on the wall lay shattered on the floor. The drapes were pulled, the lights smashed.

Her right hand traced the line of her jaw, brushed over the tiny scar shaped like a serpent swallowing its own tail. Then her fingers strayed to her neck, where the golden chain and locket no longer rested. She'd given them back to Garlotte, and with them the memento of her time with Elford, the Tzimisce fiend. Aside from the snake, the injuries to her body were healed.

Aside from the snake.

She had consumed massive quantities of blood since arriving in Baltimore, and the physical infirmities—protrusions of bone, skin stretched and fused—had become things of the past. But even as the heinous degradations of the fiends had receded, something far worse—far worse than her beauty marred!—had taken hold of her. She'd thrown herself recklessly into the petty games of politics, a vain attempt to hold her demons at bay, but after Xaviar's words two nights ago, she could no longer deny her panic. No fewer than three of her plots had come close to fruition in the past nights, and with all three, she'd missed her opportunity. Already a schism had begun to form between Prince Garlotte and Jan, yet she had failed to drive home the wedge. Then, irony of ironies, *Garlotte* himself had demanded a conclave, and she'd let the chance slip away. And then poor, gullible Fin had dared defy his sire. The prince had been embarrassed, no doubt, but had Victoria backed the childe's claim, merely spoken on his behalf—*Is this true, Alexander, that the girl has Embraced, not once but twice?*—the occasion could have been so much more.

But she had huddled in fear. Paralyzed by words that haunted her still.

Slaves of the Antediluvians.

Victoria felt a hand clutching her heart. Elford had violated her. Vykos had scarred her. But this was far more pervasive, more insidious. She placed her hand on her breast, felt for the heart that no longer beat. The fingers of her other hand traced the pattern of the finely embroidered divan beneath her, and she tried in vain to keep from trembling.

"I am not my own master," she whispered to the darkness.

Despite her fanatical quest to examine her every action, she felt the horrifying certainty that all freedom was illusory, nothing more than ignorance. Like the blood within her undead body, her soul was not her own.

Slaves of the Antediluvians.

The Final Nights are at hand.

Monday, 16 August 1999, 3:55 AM
Presidential Suite, Lord Baltimore Inn
Baltimore, Maryland

The knock of this particular hand against his door was a sound Jan had not heard before but, nonetheless, he knew the identity of his caller before Hans van Pel announced the guest.

"Mr. Bell to see you, sir."

"Show him in, of course."

A moment later, Bell filled the doorway. To the Sabbat, he was a dark angel of death; for Jan, the Brujah might yet prove the staunchest of allies. While Victoria could be outmaneuvered, and Garlotte usually prodded in the direction Jan wanted the prince to go, the Brujah was one to be dealt with forthrightly. Thankfully, that suited Jan's purposes, for he and Bell were unswerving in their loyalty to their masters—though it was common knowledge that the archon despised Justicar Pascek—and they had both been assigned the same task: turn back the Sabbat tide.

"Bad news," Bell said without preamble. "Buffalo is gone."

Jan received the shock silently

"Lladislas was okay with the plan. He'd delegated the Embracing to some nobodies and caught the last train out of town. I was more surprised than he was when the Sabbat actually attacked."

Deep in thought, Jan sat at the nearby cherrywood table. He gestured for Theo to join him. For as large a man as he was, the Brujah was surprisingly graceful in his movements. He was anything but the bull in a china shop as he eased into a seat

among the exquisite trappings of Garlotte's personal suite.
Jan had been planning for this eventuality—that Buffalo
would fall. But it had happened so *soon*. He'd been figuring
in terms of weeks, not nights. "They didn't divert forces from
Washington," Jan commented.

"They didn't need to. Those were babies with fangs they
were facing."

"But they shouldn't have known that."

"I know."

The hard gazes of the Ventrue and the Brujah met and held
steady for several seconds.

"Could it have been a raid that got lucky?" Jan asked.

"Too big for a raid. Too small for an all-out assault—unless
they knew what to expect." Bell took off his baseball cap and
tossed it onto the table. His jacket creaked with the movement
of his arm. "I...I should have stayed. I could have stopped it."

"You had no way to know. And we need you more here."
Jan's comment, though calculated for effect, was true enough.
"If only I'd convinced Garlotte to let us send at least a few
squads...."

"He wasn't about to let us take anything from here," Bell
said. "If you'd given him an ultimatum, he'd have sent you
packing. He knew your hands were tied. You couldn't go back
to Hardestadt empty-handed."

Jan had to agree. Hardestadt would have been...displeased,
to say the least. Jan also found himself surprised by Bell's
insight. *Perhaps I've been underestimating him*, Jan thought. And
perhaps that insight could be brought to bear on other matters.

"Too big for a raid," Jan repeated Theo's words from a
minute before. "Too small for an all-out assault—unless they
knew what to expect."

"That's how it looked to me." Theo crossed his arms. He sat
straight as an oak.

"Which means...?"

"They knew." Those two words from Theo carried the
impact of certainty. He'd obviously been pondering this very
question since leaving Buffalo.

The Brujah's conviction strengthened the suspicion that Jan

had been harboring for some time now, since the night of the attack on his unlife. Something that Blaine had said that night, a comment that hadn't really made sense at the time but which Jan had been too busy trying to survive to give much thought to, came back to him: *They know what you know.* Remembering those words, and hearing Theo give voice to what Jan was already thinking, made it that much easier to believe. Only one question remained?

"Who?"

Theo took his time thinking about that.

"Could it have been someone on the ground in Buffalo?" Jan asked.

"Maybe. But we ran a pretty tight damn ship," Theo said. "Nobody but me and Lladislas knew everything. I guess somebody could've figured it out."

"Possible," said Jan. "Who else...on this end?"

"Anybody who was there the night we decided," Theo answered right away this time.

Jan pictured the scarred conference table in his mind and began listing the participants from that night: "Garlotte, Gainesmil, Roughneck, yourself, me, Victoria, Vitel, Colchester, and Malachi."

"Colchester wasn't there that night," Theo corrected him. Jan raised an eyebrow. Theo sighed. "You're right," said the Brujah. "He wasn't at the table, but so what? Okay. Colchester. Fin came in too. He could've heard."

"That's a formidable list."

"Hold on," Theo said. "You're not done yet. Then add anybody that any of those folks might have talked to. That gives us, what...maybe a hundred possible spies?"

"Gainesmil has proven himself to be opportunistic," Jan suggested.

Theo shrugged. "So? Roughneck's crazy, and Victoria's a bitch. Don't prove nothing."

Jan didn't know much about Roughneck, but Victoria could not be dismissed so lightly. "Victoria was captured by the Sabbat in Atlanta. She may have been...tampered with. She could have arranged the Maria Chin assassination and sold us out on

Buffalo. Garlotte could have been trying to make sure there was no competition for Camarilla resources," Jan continued. "He's made it clear he wants everything and everyone he can get here to protect his city. Vitel?"

Theo seemed reluctant to hazard a guess, even after hearing Jan speculate about possible treachery from a fellow Ventrue. The Brujah archon shrugged at last. "Trying to get hold of Baltimore?" He shook his head. "But I don't know how Buffalo going down would do him any good. Maybe same as Garlotte, except instead of wanting everybody to protect Baltimore, Vitel wants an army to retake D.C."

Jan couldn't fault that suggestion. "That leaves Malachi—revenge for the Gangrel?"

"And maybe Colchester," Theo added. "Who the hell knows?" He was clearly frustrated by the wide range of possibilities.

And you, Jan thought. After all, Theo had been in the know about Buffalo, and he'd been on the docks the night of the assassination attempt on Jan. Coincidence? *But why would he have saved me from Blaine...? Unless he had more to gain by me trusting him.* There was no way, at present, to know for sure. But Jan would have to find out, so he hardened himself to the tasks that lay ahead.

"It was bound to happen," he said, steering the conversation back toward Buffalo, "but a few more weeks would have been nice." Jan paused and regarded the Brujah for several seconds. Theo's face was expressionless again, inscrutable as ever. "I have several ideas about how we should proceed," Jan said. "I'd like your opinion."

Theo shrugged. "I got nowhere to be."

Tuesday, 24 August 1999, 11:48 PM
Cherry Hill
Baltimore, Maryland

"Where the hell is Katrina?" Jazz yelled. Tarika answered from downstairs: "She had to go talk to her daddy!"

"Hmph." Her daddy, the high-and-mighty prince of vampires. "She oughta tell that old man to go kiss his own ass, instead of getting her to do it all the time," Jazz muttered to herself. She sighed as she pulled on her pants. The upstairs of the house was too stuffy—no wonder, with the shutters nailed shut and covered with tar paper. Katrina had been talking about boarding up the downstairs windows too. Jazz wasn't sure why. The bars kept out intruders—the curious, criminal, and stupid—and since she, Katrina, and Tarika were never downstairs during the day, the sunlight didn't really matter.

"Whatever."

Katrina would do what she wanted to, whether Jazz and Tarika liked it or not. Jazz briefly considered making the king-sized bed where the three of them spent their days, and was on the verge of deciding it would be too much trouble, when she heard some kind of crash from downstairs.

"Tarika?" Jazz started downstairs to see what the noise was. "Girl, what the hell you doing down here?"

The living room and the Naugahyde sofa were empty, but through the doorway to the kitchen Jazz could see the naked lightbulb that hung over the table swinging back and forth. She walked into the kitchen and tripped.

Several details registered in Jazz's mind at once: Tarika's

head, which Jazz had tripped on and that now bounced across the floor; the open window and bent bars; the recognizable hairy face of Malachi, one of the prince's thugs; and the bloody machete he was swinging at her.

Wednesday, 25 August 1999, 12:05 AM
U.S.S. Apollo, the Inner Harbor
Baltimore, Maryland

Garlotte sat and brooded. His three childer stood before him. The gently swaying lantern that usually soothed him was, tonight, merely another source of aggravation. He drummed his fingers on the arm of his high-backed wooden chair—the action was partially an indulgence of habit, partially calculated to irritate his audience. He knew them well, though often he saw them as he wished them to be rather than as they actually were. No more.

"Did you *want* something?" Katrina finally asked, after only an hour and a half of waiting.

Garlotte smiled. He'd known she would be the first to challenge him, but he'd hoped she might hold out longer. "Ah, Katrina, are you in such a hurry, with eternity stretching out before you?" The prince gestured toward Isaac. "You should be more like your elder brother."

Katrina sneered. "What, a pussy?"

The sheriff, to his credit, didn't respond to her taunt. Reluctantly, Garlotte rose from his seat and pulled his flowing, regal robe close to him. It was the type of attire that was useful when he wished to emphasize his authority. He stepped toward his childer and stood directly in front of Katrina, who was in the center, but when he raised his hand, it was on Isaac's left shoulder that it came to rest.

Staring intently at the girl but squeezing Isaac's shoulder, Garlotte said, "This is my son, in whom I am well pleased." *Well pleased* was somewhat of an exaggeration, but the prince had already left out *beloved*, and he hated to carry poetic license too far. Isaac was solid, if uninspiring, and he would continue to grow into the role of sheriff over the years.

Garlotte released his grip on Isaac. "And you, Fin," he said, still staring directly at Katrina. "When last we spoke, you claimed the right to Embrace your mortal girl. Though I was pleased to see you assert yourself this once, your choice of venue for that conversation was…ill-considered. Who prodded you in this decision?"

Fin hesitated, but only briefly. "Ms. Ash. She suggested…." His words trailed off quickly.

"Do you see now," asked Garlotte, "that she had motives other than your best interest? Though I have no doubt she was persuasive. Do you see it?"

Fin nodded meekly. His voice was barely audible. "I do."

"Good."

With blinding speed, Garlotte's right hand shot free of his robe and slammed a stake into the chest of his youngest childe. Before either of the others could even react, Fin staggered and collapsed to the floor.

"I reclaim this blood," said Garlotte. Not once had his eyes strayed from Katrina's face. She was struggling not to glance down at Garlotte's robe, to try to see if another weapon lurked beneath the folds, perhaps a stake meant for her.

But the prince turned from her, at last, and took three deliberate steps back to his throne. He settled himself comfortably before again taking notice of his two remaining childer. Garlotte gestured toward Fin. "His mortal is dead. I instructed Malachi to be sure she felt no pain." The prince pressed his fingertips together, making a child's steeple. "I gave him no such injunction in dealing with your…playthings, Katrina."

Her eyes grew wide with surprise and fear.

She'll hate herself for that slip, Garlotte thought. *And she'll hate me.*

"Go to them," he said, and as if his words released her from a spell, Katrina broke for the door in a dead run. A few seconds, and her footsteps receded into nothingness.

Friday, 27 August 1999, 11:52 PM
McHenry Auditorium, Lord Baltimore Inn
Baltimore, Maryland

"*What in the nine hells are you thinking?*" Prince Lladislas and his entourage, most recently of Buffalo, had been in Baltimore for just over a week. Some of that time, the deposed prince had been a quite gracious guest, but not most of the time. And not tonight. "Since Embracing a bunch of know-nothing neonates worked so damned well in Buffalo, you're going to do it again in Hartford? What's the matter with you, Garlotte? Letting these boys run wild? And Theo—"

The Brujah archon calmly and gently placed a restraining hand on Lladislas's wrist. The Brujah prince abandoned his tirade. He seemed to regard Theo with the highest esteem.

Thank God, thought Jan. Otherwise, Lladislas would be unbearable.

Theo's intervention calmed but couldn't cow Lladislas. "I'm sure you like pulling all the homeless Kindred down here so *you* have a strong city," he said to Garlotte. "Wouldn't have minded doing that myself—rather than abandoning my city."

Jan wanted to cover his eyes. He prayed that Garlotte would exercise restraint and not say something like, *We can't waste our resources in inferior cities, Prince Lladislas.*

This once, Jan's prayer was granted. "The decision has been made for the present, Prince Lladislas. If you would like to discuss the matter with Mr. Pieterzoon, Mr. Bell, and Mr. Gainesmil—at a later date…"

Lladislas tossed up his hands. He was still, Jan knew, adjusting to the role of prince-in-exile. It was a tricky thing—judging how far to press one's case when a guest in the domain of another prince, especially if there was no *home* to go home to. Aggravating as he could be, Lladislas's disgruntlement was promising in one sense—it meant that Theo had not let his fellow Brujah in on the plan to which the defense of Hartford was only the beginning. Gainesmil, too, though he'd had a hand in the strategizing, knew only so much. Secrecy was everything at this stage.

"…And you have brought information for us, Regent Sturbridge," Prince Garlotte was saying.

Sturbridge rose easily to her feet, almost without Jan realizing that she was moving. She nodded to the principals on the council: "Prince Garlotte, Archon Bell, Prince Vitel, Prince Lladislas, Mr. Pieterzoon."

The Tremere regent had spent most of the past weeks at her chantry in New York City, where she apparently felt her presence was most needed. The Camarilla portion of that city was under perpetual siege by the Sabbat, so she might well have been correct.

After the assassination of Maria Chin here in Baltimore, in this very inn, Sturbridge might have felt safer in New York as well as most needed, though if Colchester's information were accurate, the chantry was not exactly a safe haven.

Something about the woman struck Jan as…otherworldly— certainly not angelic, not necessarily demonic. But detached, aloof. Aside from acknowledging those seated in the places of honor, she might have been lecturing a group of school children, or giving directions to a lost motorist, so dispassionate were her words.

"Prince Garlotte informed me three weeks ago," she began, "of the assertions Justicar Xaviar of Clan Gangrel made to this body. Speaking officially, on behalf of Clan Tremere, we can lend no credence to his claims regarding what he characterized as an Antediluvian. I have, however, become aware of information that *may* be related to the events the justicar described." She placed a leather attache case on the table and removed a single piece of parchment, which she handed to Jan.

Staring up at him was a large eye, or rather a hastily sketched portrait of a man, unremarkable except for his left eye, which was grossly oversized and bulged from its socket.

"Who is this supposed to be?" Jan asked, then passed the parchment to the two Malkavians to his right.

"That, Mr. Pieterzoon," Sturbridge answered, "we do not know. The picture was produced under circumstances that are not completely clear at this point, but its creation coincides almost exactly with the...situation described by Justicar Xaviar." Despite Sturbridge's low-key delivery, Jan was amazed by her words. The Tremere—a regent from that most secretive and suspicious of clans—were admitting *publicly* what they did not know and even going so far as to seek the opinion of the other clans! Some might have taken this as a hopeful sign of cooperation. To Jan, it was a signpost of the dire straits of the Camarilla. If the Tremere warlocks did not see the end looming near, Sturbridge would not he here.

The parchment passed from the Malkavians to Theo and Lladislas, to Gainesmil, to Garlotte. "Is this creature Kindred or kine...or something else?"

"A reasonable question," said Sturbridge. "Again, we do not know."

The picture passed from the Prince of Baltimore to Isaac, to Colchester the businessman. "I don't know who this is, but I could find out," said the Nosferatu.

Sturbridge nodded. "We had hoped there would be a variety of resources that could be brought to bear upon this question."

Jan still marveled at her frank admission of ignorance in the matter. The phrase that, in all his years of undeath, he had never heard a Tremere utter rang in his ears: *We do not know.*

Colchester passed the leaf of parchment to Vitel, who studied it, then handed it to Victoria, seated just on the other side of Sturbridge. Victoria, still unusually withdrawn, straightened slightly in her seat. She stared intently at the picture.

What do the Tremere hope to gain from this? Jan wondered. Did they think they could divert the suspicions of the other clans by appearing inept? No, he decided, that couldn't be it. The clan had survived this long because of its strength. Other Kindred knew little about the warlocks, and what common knowledge did exist—actual or perceived—was disturbing, not comforting. Jan could not believe that the Tremere would attempt to coddle the other clans and make nice.

"Leopold."

Victoria's one word grabbed the attention of all at the table.

"This is Leopold," she said quietly, not quite believing what she saw, or what she thought she saw, on the parchment.

"You know him," said Sturbridge.

"Did his eye always look like that?" asked Roughneck, very concerned.

"Who," Prince Garlotte asked, "is Leopold?"

Victoria stared at the picture without acknowledging the prince. Jan couldn't believe that this was the same woman who had inspired such...confusion in him, and who had been such a thorn in his side. She seemed to grow smaller and weaker before his eyes.

"Who is Leopold?" Garlotte asked again.

"No one," Victoria said with a wave of her hand, not yet looking up from the picture. "A sculptor...a Toreador, from Atlanta."

From Atlanta. To Jan's thinking, too much was connected to that city to be coincidence: Victoria escaped from there after the first Sabbat attack; a Tremere was possibly assassinated; and now this sketch that might be the creature that destroyed an army of Gangrel....

Jan was struck suddenly by the absurdity of that line of reasoning. "You're not suggesting that a Toreador destroyed thirty or forty Gangrel?"

Now Victoria did look up. She stared, exasperated, at Jan. "I'm only saying," she glanced at the parchment again, "that's Leopold." She slid the sheet across the table toward Sturbridge.

"You're sure?" asked the Tremere. "As sure as you can be with a rough sketch?"

Victoria thought for a moment, then began to nod, slowly at first, then more confidently. "It...it *feels* like Leopold. I can't explain it exactly. But I'm sure."

Sturbridge nodded also, as if she understood something that escaped the others.

"Then we must find out what's going on with this Leopold," Garlotte broke in. "If he's possibly connected to whatever happened to the Gangrel, he may be responsible for Buffalo falling. He may be a tool of the Sabbat."

"He sure as hell ain't no Antediluvian," Theo Bell said, eliciting a few grim chuckles.

"I doubt we'll find Xaviar," Garlotte pressed on, "and even if we did, I doubt even more that he'd prove helpful, at this point. If the trail begins in Atlanta, then we need someone there."

Jan pounced on the opportunity by instinct. The words escaped his mouth almost before he realized he'd spoken: "Victoria, you know the city; you know this Leopold. It would make sense for you to go." He felt a vague sense of guilt immediately, but the pity he'd felt for the disturbed Toreador had given way instantly to his businessman's instinct for the kill. This was his chance to get rid of this woman who had challenged him, this woman he couldn't be near without wanting to *possess.*

Prince Garlotte, though he'd been harsh to Victoria recently, seemed to have reservations about that idea. "Would perhaps the Nosferatu be better able to—"

"The Nosferatu know Atlanta, true. But Victoria knows Leopold as well," Jan reiterated. "She has a feeling about this. I trust Ms. Ash's intuition."

Victoria didn't seem aware of the debate over her future. She stared after the sketch that now rested close to Sturbridge. Garlotte was clearly the most conflicted. For a long moment he wavered. Jan worried the prince was about to veto the suggestion.

"My prince," chimed in Gainesmil, also worried by the developments, "I must suggest—"

"That she shouldn't go alone?" Garlotte put the words in his lieutenant's mouth. "Are you volunteering to accompany her, Robert?"

Gainesmil's mouth hung open for several seconds. "I... uh...I believe...with all due respect, my prince...that perhaps my particular skills are needed here?" He obviously hadn't intended to phrase his suggestion as a question, but his voice betrayed his near-panic and the final word jumped at least an octave.

Prince Garlotte pondered the question for several moments during which Gainesmil sat perfectly still. "I suppose you are right, Robert."

Gainesmil tried not to sigh too audibly. He seemed to have salvaged his place at the prince's side, for the time being. Jan admired the prince's deft handling of the situation—almost as deft as his own. Garlotte could have agreed to Jan's suggestion, but the prince had been making an effort to curb Jan's influence, by measures such as insisting that Gainesmil had a part in strategic planning. Conversely, to protect Victoria after she'd obviously fallen out of favor and spurned Garlotte's hospitality would have been seen by many as a sign of weakness.

Gainesmil had unwittingly saved the prince. His interference allowed Garlotte to shift the focus of the decision— of course Victoria would go—to his own largesse and mercy in disciplining a wayward subject.

Jan's plan was adopted. Garlotte brought to heel the prodigal. Gainesmil was not sent on a suicide mission. Positive results, for all except—

"I will go," Victoria said, not having herself expressed an opinion on the subject until now. "I'll go. I'll find Leopold."

Jan felt another twinge of guilt. If the conduct tonight of the Tremere had been puzzling, Victoria's recent behavior was dumbfounding. Since Xaviar's appearance, she had completely abandoned her various attempts to influence the council. She had retreated from the world around her...*like Estelle*, Jan realized. Like a victim who denied that with which she could no longer cope. Suddenly, he saw Victoria in a new light—and Jan wanted to care for her, to protect her. He saw her beauty and remembered her earlier strength of will, a fire that might yet be rekindled.

But—at his urging—she was being sent back to the city she had fled, back to the Sabbat.

"Very well," said Garlotte, maintaining control of the situation. "Find this Leopold. Find out what's going on with this...this *eye*."

Jan sat back quietly in his chair. Victoria was no longer his problem. There was still the Sabbat to contend with. Prince Garlotte was a necessary, if not steadfast, ally. Jan would guide the prince where he could, and circumvent him otherwise. The weight of the world rested on Jan's shoulders. Still, his mind wandered back to Victoria and to the cruel hand he had dealt her. Of one thing he was certain—Hardestadt would be pleased.

About the Author

Gherbod Fleming has *never* been employed with or compensated in any way by the Central Intelligence Agency. He is the author of *Clan Novel: Gangrel*, as well as the Vampire: The Masquerade Trilogy of the Blood Curse—*The Devil's Advocate, The Winnowing,* and *Dark Prophecy.*

Curious about other Crossroad Press books?
Stop by our site:
http://store.crossroadpress.com
We offer quality writing
in digital, audio, and print formats.

Printed in Great Britain
by Amazon